Other books by R.K. Gleason

The True Death Series

The True Death

The Vengeful Death

The New Death

The Lonely Death

Death's Return

Death Threats

Death Match

The Bitter Years Series

Savaged

Dedication

For Petra. Thanks for being slower than me.
I'll always love you, baby...

PROLOGUE

Leading scientists have been warning for many years about the overprescribing of antibiotics to the military troops and to the public at large. Their assertion is, while the intention of the tiny microbes is to combat viruses, the long-term results are the antibiotics mutate many of the viruses at a molecular level, making them stronger and more resistant to standard treatment.

Much like the influenza virus which mutates from year to year and from patient to patient each time a person becomes infected with the flu, the virus changes slightly and adapts. Every year, a new vaccine is produced, based on an educated guess of how the prevalent viruses will behave. The pharmaceutical companies, in their infinite greed, created even stronger antibiotics which only exacerbated the problem. Combine all that, with excessively overused anti-inflammatory drugs, other pain medications, chemicals and GMOs in our food supplies, pollution, other prescription medications and over the counter cold, flu and allergy medicines. Hell, maybe even the fluoride in our water played its part. Regardless of the exact combination, the scientists warned when we started mixing all these together and then let them percolate in the human body for a decade or so, we might just discover Pandora's Box had been sleeping inside mankind all along.

Where all the great thinkers and theorists had their collective heads buried up their asses is they were only concerned with the effects on human subjects. They never altered their thinking to consider pets and add them into the equation. Fifty years ago, when Rover got sick, one of three things happened. It died. It got better. Or, you took it out behind the barn and *Old Yeller'd* its ass. But not now. In the past few decades, life has become softer for everyone. But again, no one considered what effect prolonged, aggressive medical treatments were having on domesticated animals.

The first sign of trouble was in 1986 with the discovery of *bovine spongiform encephalopathy,* commonly called mad cow disease. The cause of the disease was linked to the practice of grinding up dead animals and adding them to the food intended for the same type of animal.

In 1990, the British Agriculture Minister appeared on television, urging his four-year-old daughter to eat a hamburger and assuring the public that the beef was safe. Canada reported its first case of Mad Cow Disease in 1993 and in late 1996, the British government admitted BSE-infected beef might possibly transmit mad cow disease to humans. By then, millions of people had already been exposed to the tainted meat and another toxic component was added to the time-bomb of an ever-expanding petri dish. In 1998, the U.S. and Canada restricted the imports of any food intended for human consumption that might be tainted. It wasn't until 2003 when they finally banned all animal foods that might contain beef products from cows that were fed the remains of other dead cows. But by then, the genie may have already been let out of the bottle...

CHAPTER ONE

Eyewitness News – WCMH – November 1, 2019...

Dan Richards waits for the Channel 10 sportscaster, Clint Forest, to finish his breakdown of the college football game this weekend during his allotted four-and-a-half-minute sports update portion of the eleven o'clock news half-hour. The *Breaking News* text had flashed onto Dan's teleprompter at the beginning of Clint's recap of the big game this weekend. As the news anchor for the last two years, it's Dan's job to deliver the urgent stuff. But after reading through it, he decides to wait for Clint to finish his section, before cutting off the little snot, Katy Cho. The station hired the perky little bitch six months ago to co-host the evening news with Dan. They told him demographic research showed women viewers related to Katy and viewership had increased a full two points since she'd started. Dan hadn't been quiet about his belief viewership had increased more because of Katy's huge tits rather than anyone *relating* to her. Dan was certain it was male viewers who had increased the show's ratings, because they tuned in every night in the hopes of a wardrobe malfunction. Dan could tell from her very first day, the former cheerleader was after his job. But he'd been in the news business for the last twenty-seven years. He took care of himself, eating healthy and working out five days a week. His hair had just enough gray at the temples to look distinguished, or as Dan liked to believe, sexy without looking like someone's grandfather, which he was. There was no way he was going to let a walking, talking pair boobs steal the career he'd scraped and clawed to build.

"And that's the way I see it," Clint says, delivering his signature sign-off at the end of his piece and bringing Dan back to the moment. "Back to you Katy."

"This just in to our station," Dan says into *Camera 3*, interrupting Katy before she can start her thirty seconds of throw away, feel-good story. It's the usual shlock the station likes them to sign-off from the news with, but not this evening. While Dan certainly doesn't consider this breaking news, it does allow him a reason to put that ladder climbing bitch in her place. "Authorities in the Hilliard area have reported one or more packs of dogs, possibly infected with a form of rabies, have been spotted. Authorities haven't specified the number of dogs or the size of the packs, but they caution residents to be on the lookout for any unattended dogs in their area. Authorities are also instructing citizens not to approach these animals, as the dogs are reported to be extremely aggressive toward humans. Authorities say you should instead, notify the local Animal Protection Agency, whose number is at the bottom of our screen."

"This really makes you wonder, who let the dogs out," Clint says as they cut to him with *Camera 4*, just in time to see him pump his open hands into the air and say, "Woof, woof, woof woof..."

"Right you are, Clint," Dan says, effectively eating all the time allotted for Katy's *things aren't so bad* piece at the end of the show. "For Katy, Clint, and myself... Good night Columbus, and have a great tomorrow."

CHAPTER TWO

"THAT WAS THE dumbest ending I've ever seen!" Dave says to his wife, referring to the movie they just watched as he glares at their ridiculously huge, 72-inch television.

"That's hardly the dumbest movie you've ever watched," Pam replies.

"You liked that movie?" he asks.

"Oh, hell no," she says. "I'm just saying you've watched way stupider shit than that!"

David and Pamela Richter gave up on regular cable less than two years ago after realizing all they ever watched were horror movies and cooking shows. They could watch most any of those on a variety of subscription-based, streaming channels on the internet. In fact, they didn't even listen to the radio any longer because they had *Spotify* for that. Although, they usually listened to audiobooks in the car. Dave felt completely empowered when he made the call to their cable TV provider, telling them to take a high hard one and canceled their account. After thirty minutes on the phone and two separate transfers to different customer service reps, he'd finally been connected with a supervisor named Christopher, who sounded like he was all of seventeen years old.

"Mr. Richter, you understand you'll be losing all of your local and national channels? Including local news and sports,"

Christopher had advised.

"I don't watch sports," Dave repeated, having received the same cautionary warning from the previous two CSRs.

"But what about local and national news?" Christopher had asked. "You'll be missing out on current events."

"I don't give a shit!" Dave shouted into his cell phone, having reached his breaking point.

"Let me take a look at your current plan and see if there's something I can offer you," Christopher said.

"Goddamn it, Chris!" Dave said.

"It's Christopher, Mr. Richter," he interrupted.

"What the fuck ever! I don't want your cable, your phone or anything from you guys! I know you're just doing your job, but I'm done."

"If it's about the amount of your bill, Mr. Richter," Christopher continued undaunted. "I can offer you the same package you have now, plus three movie channels without increasing your bill. In fact," he says, clacking away on his keyboard from some other part of the world. "I can give you all that, and actually reduce your bill by seven dollars a month if you agree to a two-year contract. How would that be?"

"You're not, fucking, listening to me," Dave yelled, pulling the phone away from his ear to shout directly at the tiny screen. "All I ever watch are clown movies and chicken porn! Now turn all my shit off!" He didn't really watch chicken porn, but he'd thrown it in with the hope of shocking the corporate dweeb out of his script and into submission.

"Oh, I see. Hold please," Christopher said, putting Dave on hold before he could protest.

"Don't put me on hold!" Dave shouted into the muted line.

"Chicken porn?" Pam asked. She'd watched the whole farcical process since he'd started the call.

"If he transfers me to some other asshole, I'm going to lose my shit," Dave tells her, ignoring her question.

"*Going* to lose your shit? The grip on your shit is always tenuous at best and you set that shit free when you were transferred the first time. Chicken porn..." she says, shaking her head with a grin.

"Do you want to do this?" he asks, trying to hand her the phone.

"Not now," Pam says, pushing the cell phone away. "I'm not jumping in now! Not to be the wife of the chicken fucker!"

"I'm not fucking chickens!" he shouts.

"Mr. Richter?" Christopher asks quietly from the other end of the line, obviously having heard Dave's animated denial of bestiality.

"Fuck me..." Dave sighs.

"Pardon me, sir."

"Nothing. Are we done?"

"I've completed your request for cancellation and I terminated your services while I had you on hold. I must inform you the cancellation won't be complete until you return all the equipment to one of our local offices. Until then, you'll continue to be billed for the rental charges."

"Of course, we will," Dave sighed, squeezing his cell phone in frustration.

"Would you like the address of our closest office to you?"

"I know where it is."

"Is there anything else I can do for you today?"

"Fuck off, Chris," Dave said as he ended the call.

Needless to say, Pam laughed her ass off when Dave discovered he couldn't get any other internet provider to run a line into their apartment and was forced to call *Comcast* back to get everything turned back on. Dave was furious the signal pirates wouldn't offer him the same sweet deals to get him back as a customer as they had trying to keep him from disconnecting the service in the first place. Pam laughed when he asked to speak to a manager about the injustice, certain the supervisor would review Christopher's notes on the account and give special consideration to Dave's parting comments. Pam wasn't nearly as amused when he told her they couldn't reinstall the wireless router until the following Thursday.

"I'm not sure what you expected," Pam says, referring to the eighty-seven minutes of cinematic disappointment they'd just endured. "Shudder only gave it two skulls."

"That's two out of five," Dave replies like he has a valid argument. "You know horror movies always get low ratings."

"It's a horror channel."

"And your point is?"

"Shudder *made* the fucking movie," she says with a laugh.

"Meaning theirs is the last opinion we should trust," Dave says with a grin. "Do you want an update?" he asks, changing the subject as he shakes the cubes in his empty tumbler and stands from the couch.

"Yes, please," Pam says before draining most of her drink. Swallowing the last gulp, she hands him her glass with an inch of watered-down vodka and tonic with a splash of cranberry and a few slivers of floating ice.

"You want me to dump this?"

"No need."

"Seriously?" he asks, looking at the light pink liquid.

"It's good," she assures him with a dismissive wave.

"Okay," Dave replies, shaking his head as he goes into the kitchen to make fresh drinks. Setting the glasses on the counter, he looks at his wife's glass again, knowing the inch of old beverage is going to water-down the new one. "Fuck it," he mutters, dumping it in the sink.

"I said you didn't have to dump that," Pam calls from the couch.

"It's a small price to pay for your happiness, dear," he replies, blowing her a kiss.

"I love you," she says, blowing one back.

"You're just saying that because I'm making cocktails."

"No! I'd tell you that even if you weren't making cocktails. The fact that you are, only makes me love you more," Pam says with a grin.

"I'm going to spit in it."

"Don't even think about it," Pam says, suddenly dead serious.

"No shit?" Dave asks as he starts to laugh.

"That's not funny," she replies.

"Seriously? We've been married for all these years and have had our mouths and tongues on every nook and cranny of each other, but your hard limit is my saliva in your drink?"

"Like I said, don't even think about it," Pam warns again.

"I should've rubbed my dick around the rim," he says, handing Pam her fresh, spit-free cocktail.

"Maybe on the next one," she replies, blowing him another kiss before taking a sip.

"Harlot."

"Tramp," she says, gently setting her glass on the end table.

"Are you about ready for bed?" Dave asks, glancing at the clock under the TV, showing it's a few minutes after ten.

"You just made fresh beverages," Pam says, looking at him with annoyed disbelief.

"I meant after these."

"We'll see," she replies. "I mean it's Friday night."

"And we're so old," Dave adds.

In the last ten years, the couple had only been up past midnight a couple dozen times, and they could both count on one hand the mornings they'd slept in past six-thirty in the last twelve months. Even on the weekends, they just seemed to always get up around five in the morning and tried to be done with all of their running around and errands by early morning. Then they could usually fuck off the rest of the day and get to the other things they had planned.

"There goes another siren," Pam says, hearing the warning in the distance getting louder. "I wonder what's going on tonight?"

"Well," Dave says, walking over to the window and looking through the blinds of their third-floor walkup. "It is a game weekend, so there's probably a lot going on at the campus. All the trucks have been heading that direction."

Neither of them follows, or even likes, sports much. But, living in Columbus, knowing when the state university's playing football games at home, is a matter of survival. You had to know which streets to stay away from to avoid getting stuck in traffic. Or which areas near the campus would have a high police presence, due to frat-boy shenanigans. So, it's just common sense to pay attention to the schedule, whether you ever plan on attending a game or not.

"If the natives are this restless the night before the game, there's going to be some car-door slamming on campus tomorrow."

"And probably some couch burning in the streets if they lose," Dave says, turning away from the window and taking a sip of his cocktail.

"And only slightly less if they win," Pam adds, lifting her own glass in a toast with a grin.

"College kids," Dave says, shaking his head. "I mean, what the fuck?"

"I know, right?"

"Are you about ready for bed, gorgeous?" Dave asks again.

"In a few minutes," Pam replies, looking at her half-full cocktail. "You can go without me if you want to."

"Actually," he says, picking up his pack of cigarettes and disposable lighter.

"You're going to go outside and smoke," Pam says, finishing his sentence.

"Yep," he replies, stuffing the items into the pants pocket of his pajamas and bending down to kiss Pam. "I love you," he says as he stands.

"I love you too, baby. Don't forget to grab the keys before you go outside."

The apartment they've lived in for two years is on the third floor of a building located in the city's art district. Because it's an apartment, there's no smoking inside, which Dave usually abides by. The heavy door to their apartment, and all the others in the building, are set to automatically lock when they close. And, from their apartment, it's just a short walk to the back exit which leads to the fire escape. Dave keeps a shitty plastic chair, an ashtray, and a cement cinderblock for a makeshift table, behind the door and out of the way outside.

"Got 'em," he replies shaking the small ring of keys at Pam before heading to the door. "I'll be back in a few minutes."

"I should be ready for bed when you come back," Pam says, taking another sip of her drink.

"Cool," Dave says, blowing her a kiss and stepping into the hallway.

As soon as Dave steps outside onto the narrow, fire escape landing, he hears more sirens in the distance, all coming from the north, near the campus. He can also hear the traffic noise from the street below. Because he's at the rear of the building, a lot of the noise is usually filtered out by the structure itself. Dave's gotten used to the college crowd revving the engines to their motorcycles as they sit at a traffic light, and groups of wandering drunk girls screaming at each other from the corners. But, tonight's sounds are filled with more horn honking and tire screeching than usual. Enjoying his last smoke of the day, he decides it's not all that different from most game weekend nights until he sees a helicopter circling in the air to the north.

"Fucking college kids," he says. Exhaling the smoke through his nose, Dave crushes out his cigarette in the overflowing ashtray and heads back inside.

CHAPTER THREE

"Do you want some coffee?" Dave asks, lying awake in their bed at four forty-five in the morning.

"That would be awesome," Pam says groggily as she rubs her eyes.

"I don't suppose you feel like making it?"

"You're the one that offered, dick!"

"It wasn't technically an offer," he replies. Swinging his legs out of bed, he scratches his stomach before rubbing his face with both hands. "Technically, I was just checking to see if you wanted some, but that's cool. I've got it."

"Thank you, baby," Pam says, reaching for the lamp on her nightstand. "Lights," she warns before switching it on.

"Fuck!" Dave says, squinting through slits and shielding his eyes.

"Do you want me to help you with the coffee?" Pam asks. They both know she doesn't really mean it and she's only asking as a gentle way of reminding Dave to *go make the fucking coffee*.

"I said I've got it," he mutters, stepping into his pajama pants and pulling them up to his waist.

"Did the sirens keep you up all night too?" Pam asks, shouting her question from their bedroom.

"No shit! I think I heard the last one about two-thirty," he replies.

"Huh? I can't hear you!" she shouts back.

"I said, if you want to talk to me, then come out here," he says, shouting it loud enough for her to hear.

"I'll wait," she answers cheerfully.

"Yeah. That's what I thought," Dave mutters as he starts making coffee. Eight minutes later, he's delivering a steaming cup of strong coffee, with a spoonful of sugar and a splash of cream, to her nightstand. "Here, you bloodsucker," he says.

"I said I would help," Pam replies innocently, looking up from her Kindle.

"Not really. I'm going to the grocery store after this cup," he says, blowing her a kiss before heading to the door with his own mug.

"I'll be ready," she says, throwing the covers back in disgust.

"You don't have to go."

"Yeah. But you won't get any of the right stuff at the store," Pam tells him.

"Either way, I'm not going until I finish this," Dave says, lifting the mug to his lips.

"Whatever," Pam replies, shuffling into the bathroom connected to their bedroom and closing the door.

"Seriously," he says, walking over to lean on the doorframe. "You don't have to go if you don't want to."

"I'm up now," Pam shouts over the sound of her peeing.

"Suit yourself," Dave says to the door as he hears the toilet flush.

Ten minutes later, they're both dressed, teeth brushed and stepping into the hallway of their apartment building.

"Have you got the keys?" Pam asks with Dave standing in the doorway.

"Yes," he says automatically as he looks down at his empty hands. "Shit. Wait. I do now," he tells her after disappearing back into the apartment.

"That was close," she tells him as Dave closes the door. They'd only locked themselves out of their apartment one time since moving in. That time, it took Dave all of five minutes to slide open one of the two low, guestroom windows that faced onto the fire escape. He put wooden dowels in both the next day, making it impossible for anyone else to perform his breaking and entering trick, without having to bust the glass to get in. On the other hand, he had locked himself out countless times going out for a smoke. On most of those occasions, he'd called Pam on her cell phone and pleaded with her to unlock the door and let him in.

"Nah," Dave replies, feeling his pocket for his smokes. "Damn it!" he says, ratting the key into the lock and disappearing back into the apartment.

"Seriously," Pam says from the hallway.

"I'm ready," he tells her, closing the door with his keys in one hand and his smokes and lighter in the other.

"Are you sure?" Pam asks.

"Yes!"

"Do you have your wallet?"

"Yes," he spontaneously replies before slapping his back pocket to check.

"Do you?" she asks.

"Yes," Dave says, pushing past her and out onto the fire escape.

The parking lot for their apartment building, and the other two buildings next to theirs, is located behind their building. So, while their building has a front door facing the main street, it's always more convenient to enter and exit the building from the fire escape that leads directly down to the cars. The three buildings all have shops, restaurants or bars that occupy the first floors, with the apartments making up the second and third floors. Theirs is the smallest of the three buildings, only having a total of four apartments on each of the upper floors. Dave and Pam chose the spacious, two-bedroom apartment on the third floor to avoid any possible neighbor-noise from people living above them.

Dave navigates the narrow metal stairs with Pam following behind him. They make the turn onto the second floor and head back the other direction along a catwalk. Then, around the corner of the building to get to the next set of stairs that lead to the parking lot.

"Wow," Dave says when the lot comes into view. There are a dozen or so cars parked there, but well over half the spaces are empty.

"The parking lot's a little light this morning," Pam says as they start down the stairs.

"No kidding. I thought it might be kind of empty this morning, what with the game and all. But I wasn't expecting it to be empty!"

"It's not empty," Pam says. "I'm sure people are just starting their tailgating parties early."

"It's like, five o'clock in the fucking morning," Dave replies, glancing at his wristwatch before remotely unlocking their vehicle from the top of the stairs.

"Maybe they started yesterday?" Pam says as they descend the sixteen steps to the lot and head for their car.

They drive one of those, *not-an-SUV*, SUVs. Basically, just a small sport utility vehicle shell, mounted on a regular car chassis. The kind anyone who knows anything about off-roading would never dream of taking off road.

"Shit," Dave sighs after getting in and closing his door.

"What?"

"Did you grab your phone?" he asks.

"Don't you have yours?"

"What do you think?"

"I left mine on the table because I thought you had yours!" Pam replies.

"I'll run back up and get one," Dave says, opening his door.

"Just leave them," Pam disagrees, setting her hand on his arm before he can get out. "It's not like we need one or anything. We're just going to the store. But you do have your wallet, right?"

"Of course," he answers, involuntarily feeling for it in his back pocket again.

"Are you sure?" Pam asks with a grin.

"Bite me," he says with a chuckle, shutting his door and checking again before starting the car. "I thought there'd be more traffic," he says after a few blocks.

"It is only a few minutes after five."

"Yeah. I guess I just figured with all the partying and sirens from last night, there'd be more people in town or something."

"Like I said, it's still dark out," Pam says, right before she's thrown toward the dash of the car, her seatbelt holding her back as Dave slams on the breaks and crushes the horn.

"You bitch!" he yells.

"What the fuck?" Pam asks, glaring at Dave.

"It wasn't me! It was her," he says, pointing at the car that suddenly appeared in front of them. "She totally blew the light and just cut me off! Asshole!" he yells, slamming on the horn again.

"Stop tailgating her!"

"I'm not!"

"I'm just saying, you're pretty fucking close!"

"I know she's close, I damn near hit her," he replies, as the young woman driving the Lexus gives an obligatory wave behind her to them. The kind of wave that says *sorry, but not really, so fuck you.*

"I said *you're* too close."

"What do you want me to do, stop? She cuts us off and then does," Dave says, pausing to glance at his speedometer. "Twenty-four miles an hour. Oh! Are you fucking kidding me?" he shouts as the blonde signals to turn into the same mega-mart parking lot they're headed to.

"Do not park next to her," Pam says.

"Oh, hell no! She'd probably get out, swing her car door into ours and then just drive off," he says, parking two aisles over from the young woman.

Looking in her mirror, Pam sees the woman's taillights flash before her door opens and she slides from her car. Pam feels an instant dislike for the woman. Thin and in her late twenties, her long straight hair pulled through the back of her ballcap into a ponytail. She's wearing one of those neon colored jogging suits that's made with an excessive amount of spandex to show off the ass she's obviously spent hours in the gym to sculpt. Pam looks down at her early-fifties body, clad in jeans, a hoodie and Chuck Taylors and then back into the mirror as Dave quickly shuts off the car, pops his seatbelt and opens his door.

"Hey!" he shouts to the young woman as he stands in his open door.

"Dave! Don't!" Pam shouts at him as she scrambles to unfasten her belt.

"What?" he asks, looking into the car.

"Just let it go," Pam replies. Freeing herself from the seatbelt and opening her own door.

"But she drives like shit!" Dave replies.

He's speaking to Pam but aiming the comment at the young woman walking away from her car and making sure he's loud enough for her to hear. The woman stops and turns his direction and makes eye contact with Dave. Frowning, she turns to her car and thumbs the button on her remote. The car's alarm whoops twice and the headlights flash, indicating it now has all the security afforded Fort Knox.

"What the fuck?" Dave says after the woman looks at him one more time before turning toward the grocery store. "Did you see that shit?" he asks Pam.

"Just let it go," she says, closing her car door.

"Some people's fucking kids," he mutters, shaking his head as he checks his pockets for the keys before closing his car door. Finding them absent, he leans in and sees them still in the ignition. He leans in to grab them at the same time he hears the woman scream. While he can't see her, he knows it must be her, because she and Pam are the only other people in the parking lot and he can still see Pam through the passenger window. He quickly stands and looks over the top of the car to see the woman on the ground with a large, shaggy-looking dog jerking and shaking her left leg from the grip its jaws have on her calf.

Pam starts to head for the woman when Dave's mind snaps into action.

"Pam! Wait!" he shouts. "Get in the car and call *911*." Leaning back into the car, he pops up the center-console armrest and snatches the collapsible baton from the deep storage compartment below it. Jerking off the nylon case, he tosses it onto the seat and flicks his wrist to extend the club. Glancing down, he wishes it was longer and possibly fired bullets.

"I don't have my phone!" Pam reminds him.

"Then just get in the fucking car!" he shouts, forcing his fifty-four-year-old, out of shape and more than a few pounds overweight body into a sprint toward the downed woman. Pam moves around the front of the car to stand at the open driver's side door for a better view.

"Be careful!" she shouts.

"Just get in the fucking car!" he repeats over his shoulder.

Dave can hear the dog growling over the woman's screams as he gets closer. "Get out of here!" he yells at the dog, doing his best to sound menacing and lifting his arms to look large and intimidating. He hopes that's all he needs to do is scare the dog off. Just be loud and big, but this dog is pretty good sized and it's ignoring Dave's shouts. It hadn't looked as big from his car, but as he runs up, he sees the dog looks like it's pushing a solid fifty pounds. It doesn't sound like much, but Dave knows fifty pounds of jaw-snapping muscle and claws can seriously fuck him up if he's not careful.

He hears Pam start their car and glances over to see the reverse lights flare on. He can't help wondering if she plans to help by threatening to run them over with the car.

The dog shakes its head again, trying to tear a chunk of

meat free from the screaming woman's leg. Thick strings of the dog's saliva, turned pink from the woman's blood, fly from its mouth as it jerks its maw from side to side. The sight makes Dave rethink the car option as he raises the baton and hesitates, noticing for the first time the dog's fur is a mosaic of matted hair. Like the snarling beast has been rolling in molasses, or something equally dark and sticky. Mucousy looking tears flow from its eyes in glistening rivulets. They get lost as they mingle with the foam dripping from the dog's jaws and then are flung off in sticky ribbons as the beast thrashes.

The woman screams again as Pam's headlights spill across Dave's back, the sudden change jolting him into action. He brings the baton down across the dog's ribs as he releases a guttural yell. The dog doesn't act like it even felt the blow, and doesn't react, other than adjusting its weight on its back paws. Dave rears back again, this time aiming for the neck. He doesn't want to kill the damn thing, just make it let go. The woman screams again, a second before he brings the club down across the dog's neck, certain it'll release its hold and run off. The dog yelps through a muzzle full of leg but still refuses to let go. Dave raises the steel baton again, preparing to crack the fucking thing in the skull.

The hellhound must have sensed the blow coming because a microsecond before Dave's swing connects, it releases its hold and darts back. Unable to pull his swing in time, Dave hits the woman across her freshly chewed leg with his club, causing her to shriek again. Dave jerks back, seeing the dog hasn't made a break for it. Instead, it's focused its attention on him. The beast stands there, head lowered, and front paws spread for attack. Its haunches are tucked and coiled, ready to lunge forward and then claw backward once its jaws have sunk into Dave's flesh.

"Fuck you!" Dave shouts, jerking the baton over his shoulder and wishing he'd held his ground with Pam about getting his conceal/carry permit. Dave doesn't have anything against guns. The truth is, he actually has a tremendous respect for them. He believes in tougher gun restrictions and registration. But he doesn't think the average citizen needs an assault rifle, or semi-automatic, ever. Pam's the one with the real issue with guns. So, when Dave brought up the idea of getting his permit so he could carry a firearm, and Pam basically lost her shit, he let it go. After all, it's not like he ever found himself in a situation where he *needed* a gun, at least not until now. The dog releases a low growl and begins edging its way to the left, never taking its eyes from Dave.

"Oh! Fuck you!" Dave shouts when he realizes the thing's trying to get into a better position for attack. At this point, he's totally on board with hitting it with the car, and possibly backing over it a few times. He swings the baton again and the dog lunges away, avoiding the blow intended for its skull and spins around, jaws snapping and spraying more pink threads. Dave swings back around, hard. He's fueled by adrenaline from the anger and panic of knowing the fucking thing is trying to eat him. Pam honks the horn as she shifts into drive, distracting the dog a second before Dave cracks it across the skull with the steel bar. The dog's legs buckle and scramble for purchase as its head bounces off the pavement. Its paws twitch for a half-second as its overheated brain tries to regain control before it rolls to its feet as Pam's headlights bear down in it.

"Yeah!" Dave cheers after stepping to the side to give Pam a better angle. "Smash the fucker!" he yells just as the dog slips from Pam's crosshairs and runs off into the dark.

"What the fuck?" Pam shouts from the open car window as she crushes the brakes and slams the car into park before throwing open her door. "Did you see that shit?" she asks, looking over the hood in the direction the dog disappeared.

"Help me, please," the woman on the ground moans, getting both of their attention.

"Shit!" Pam says, seeing the amount of blood for the first time as she kneels by the woman she'd instantly disliked less than five minutes ago. "Give me your shirt!" she tells Dave.

"Do you all need some help?" an older woman shouts from just outside the store's double sliding doors.

"Call *911*!" Dave yells as he pulls his t-shirt over his head and hands it to Pam. "Get an ambulance!"

"I already tried," the woman wearing the smock with the store's logo replies. "The lines are busy."

"Try again!" Dave says as Pam ties his shirt around the woman's leg.

"Did that too," the checker answers, still not leaving the safety of the open doors.

"What the hell?" Dave says, looking down at Pam and the bleeding woman. Her color's turning an unhealthy shade of gray and she's definitely going into shock.

"She's going to be fucked if she doesn't get some help soon," Pam tells him as she tries to apply more pressure to the leg.

"There's a 24-hour, stat-care clinic about two blocks down," the clerk shouts, pointing down the street.

"How fucked?" Dave asks Pam, weighing the options against coating his backseat in the woman's blood.

"Uppercase fucked," Pam replies, jerking the knot tighter on the woman's leg before grabbing her under the arms. "Help me!" she tells him, making the decision for him.

"Right!" he says, moving to the other side so they can each take an arm. The woman sobs, weeping groggy tears. He holds the woman up as Pam slides into the back first, and he can't help noticing the bloody handprint she leaves on the door's armrest, and the back of the driver's headrest... and across the rear seat. "Goddamn it," he mutters, easing the woman through the door as Pam pulls her the rest of the way into the car. A thick coating of crimson soaks wetly into the back seat as he slams the door and jumps into the driver's seat.

"Hurry," Pam urges from the back as Dave glances down at his pack of cigarettes sitting in the console.

"I am," he replies, shifting the car into gear and wondering how pissed she'd be if he tried to light a smoke during the short, frantic drive to the *all-hours doc-in-a-box*. Deciding against it for now, he races to the exit and turns right onto the street.

"Fuck!" he shouts, slamming on the brakes for the red light at the first intersection.

"It's five o'clock in the morning," Pam reminds him. "Just run it!"

Looking in both directions and seeing one set of headlights several hundred yards to his right, Dave takes his foot from the brake pedal and stomps on the gas. As he crosses the intersection, he catches a glimpse of blue lights starting to flash above the headlights he'd seen.

"It fucking figures," he says, continuing to accelerate. Dave knows the clinic is just another block, having been there once for a cold that wouldn't go away and had worked its way into a case of pneumonia a year ago. He figures he'll get there just as, or slightly after, the police try to pull him over. Hopefully by then, they'll figure out what's going on, not write him a ticket and possibly hunt the rabid dog down and shoot it for him. All in appreciation for the good-Samaritan shit he and Pam were doing right now. Not to mention the money it was going to take to get the woman's DNA removed from the inside of their car.

Dave just gets to the parking lot entrance of the short strip mall that's home for the clinic, as the police car rounds the corner and accelerates toward him. There're more cars in here than he expected at this hour and pulls up in front of the doors. He hadn't put on his seatbelt to begin with, so it doesn't slow him down when he jumps from the car and rushes inside, shoving the swinging glass door open and banging it against the wall.

"Sir!" a stout-looking woman wearing blue scrubs and sitting behind a short, authoritarian counter says as Dave's eyes dart around the surprisingly full lobby. He spots what he needs a few feet away and rushes to it.

"Sir! You can't just take that!" the woman yells with a heavy Slavic accent as police lights begin washing through the clinic's windows, illuminating everything in blue waves. Dave grabs the handles of the wheelchair and spins it around, banging the footrests off the glass entrance and pushing the chair in front of him and out the door. Pam already has her door open having surrendered to the police. The uniformed officers appear to be grasping the bigger picture as they re-holster their tasers.

"Ma'am," one of the officers says to Pam as he helps her from the car.

"Sir. If you could please keep a steady hold on the wheelchair," the other officer says firmly to Dave while reaching down to flip on the brake for one of the wheels.

"Officers! Stop that man!" the woman from inside yells, having finally made it out from behind her receptionist's fortress of solitude.

"We have everything under control, ma'am," one of the officer's replies as he and his partner pull the bleeding woman from the car and gently set her in the wheelchair.

"Please hold the door open for us," he tells *Helga* from the clinic as he comes around and nudges Dave out of the way. "We've got it from here, sir," his partner says. "But don't leave until we've had a chance to get your statement." The officer driving the wheelchair gives it a shove and the chair pivots in place, driving a deep scratch into the paint on the lower panel of Dave's car door, with one of the footrests.

"Hey!" Dave shouts, reaching down to flip the brake off the same officer had set a few seconds ago.

"Sorry about that, sir," the officer says. "We'll be sure to add that to our report."

"Does that mean the department's going to pay for the repair?" Dave asks.

"Most likely not," his partner replies as the duo pushes past him and into the clinic.

Ninety minutes later, the sun has peeked up over the horizon. *Starsky & Hutch*, having recorded the details and taken their statements, have left the scene. Dave and Pam have convinced *Fraulein Helga*, from the receptionist's desk, they're not signing shit or being financially responsible for fuck all. They've moved the car from in front of the clinic and are sitting quietly in one of the parking spaces as Dave smokes.

"Well, that was something," Pam says, breaking the silence.

"It was that," Dave replies, looking in the rearview mirror at the brown stains smeared across the backseat beginning to turn crusty. He takes another drag before tossing the butt out the open window and looking down at his shirtless chest. "I think I'm going to suggest we skip the store this morning," he says before turning the key in the ignition.

"We're out of coffee," Pam reminds him.

"We'll come back later," he tells her as he backs out of the stall and heads for home.

CHAPTER FOUR

"THE FIRST REPORTS are coming in now," Staff Sergeant Jorje Riguez reports to Major Carolyn Brooks, standing in the communications room. Riguez intentionally left off the obligatory "sir" because he could never read how higher-ranking female officers reacted to that term of respect. A few he'd run into in the past had dressed him down in front of his platoon for the infraction. Wanting to know *if they looked like a sir* to him. Others had insisted he use the moniker, telling him they'd earned that respect. Now he just avoided it unless they insisted one way or the other. Fortunately, Major Brooks had never forced the issue in the last three years he'd been reporting to her.

"And what are they saying?" Brooks replies, fighting the urge to nervously bite her lower lip. A habit she's suppressed for the last twelve years. Her own major at the time, a hardcore lifer named Charles Beaurite had told her, *"No soldier is going to like taking orders from a woman. Especially one who reminds them of their little sister and looks like she's always second-guessing her decisions and ready to jump out of her skin."* The old man had been right, as he always had been, and she knew that single piece of advice had played a part in her last three promotions. She still reported to Beaurite, now the Bird Colonel in command of U.S. Army Base Bolivar in Southeastern Ohio.

"They're pretty sketchy, Major," Riguez answers, avoiding

the gender issue out of habit.

"Sketchy how?" she asks.

"Forgive my language, Major, but some of them sound like pure bullshit."

"Staff Sergeant. I'm going to ask this question again and this time, I want a straight, clear answer. Understood?" Brooks commands.

"Yes, Major," Riguez barks, snapping to attention.

"What are the reports?" Brooks asks, speaking each word slowly through clenched teeth.

"We've received numerous reports throughout the night, of rabid dogs attacking people," Riguez says in a loud voice, keeping his eyes focused on the far wall. "The first report was of a lone attack occurring sometime around fifteen-hundred hours yesterday. It happened in the Hilliard area, just outside of Columbus. The original reports state the animal showed no fear of people and was highly more aggressive than what is normally seen in rabid dogs."

"I know all that," Brooks says. "That's what prompted us to follow the incident. Tell me something I don't know."

"Right, Major. That first attack was like setting off a starting gun for the others. Since then, there have been multiple reports of packs attacking large groups of people in public places and single dog attacks all over the area. Spreading out and filtering into the Columbus area. We've just started receiving reports of family pets turning on their owners. One minute they're taking Fido out for a walk in the park, and the next the bastard suddenly goes rabid and bites their owner in the middle of playing fetch."

"Are the attacks limited to a specific breed? Something we

can identify and contain?"

"No, Major. Our reports say it's all breeds and we've started receiving a few reports of cats doing the same thing," Riguez answers.

"Are local authorities and Animal Control able to keep on top of this?" Brooks asks.

"Not a chance, Major. The number of reported attacks surpassed their capacity for containment about fourteen hours after the first encounter was reported."

Brooks is already familiar with the preliminary reports on the infection. The first case was identified northeast of Toledo, Ohio in the small town of Bryan. That was the initial strain when the virus was just getting ramped up. The first animal was a twelve-year-old spaniel mix named Chandler, of all things. The little bastard's owners were the typical, middle-aged yuppies with too much annual income and no children to spend it on. Meaning, Chandler lived like Lord Chandler and the couple spared no expense for their little darling. They fed the dog all that high-end, designer dog food when they weren't cooking meals for the damned thing. Taking it to the vet when it had so much as a tiny eye-booger from sleeping and insisting their vet prescribe doggie-antibiotics.

According to the records from the vet, Chandler had been prescribed a total of forty-three separate medications during his short, pampered existence. This didn't even include all the required, obligatory and unnecessary vaccinations they'd subjected their only fur-baby to. But it did include two daily scripts for anxiety meds and another to treat the high cholesterol for their wee beastie. So, it came as little surprise when the couple, a Mr. & Mrs. Manchester, rushed canine-zero back to the vet when they reported the king of the house had a slight cough. The vet, a Dr. William Faress, went through his usual, and now well-practiced, motions with the couple. He drew a precautionary sample of blood, after applying a topical, numbing ointment at the Manchester's demand, and sent it off to the lab. After performing a cursory examination of the dog, he assured them the cough they heard was most likely due to a stray hair in the dog's throat, or something equally as benign. But the couple was planning a trip to Zanesville in two days to see the wife's family and did not want their tiny bundle of fur experiencing any discomfort during the three-and-a-half-hour car ride across Ohio. The couple told the vet, should anything happen to their sweet Chandler, all they'd have to do is convince a court the vet had refused to treat the dog when they came to him in their hour of need. Then they'd ruin him. So, despite the vet's better judgment, he prescribed another course of high-spectrum antibiotics and anti-inflammatories, under duress, to avoid the Manchester's threats of a lawsuit.

Two days later, the couple's vehicle was found deep in the trees along Highway 33, just outside of Dublin, Ohio. The Subaru Outback was wrapped around a tree and burning out of control.

Once the flames were extinguished, and after a *thorough* investigation, the Ohio State Patrol wrote off the accident as follows. Mr. Manchester fell asleep at the wheel after driving from his home for *nearly* two hours and drove off the road, crashing into the large oak. The authorities say the couple rode that roller coaster off the road and into the trees, all while being safely strapped into their seatbelts at the time of the accident and were killed on impact. There was no sign of their beloved

Chandler and the State Patrol presumed the pet had been thrown from the car and died in the surrounding brush, but no search was ever made for the dog.

At some point, dripping gas from the fuel line caused by the accident, ignited on the hot engine and the vehicle caught fire, burning the couple's remains. A check of Mr. Manchester's blood for drugs or alcohol came back negative but the coroner reported the couple showed signs of multiple small animal bites. The OSP explained this as having taken place during the short span of time between the couple's crash and the car catching fire.

In the meantime, the results from the dog's blood work had come back from the lab the day after the couple's visit, but the vet put off reading them until the following morning. It wasn't until that afternoon when Dr. Faress finally *did* read the report, showing serious signs of some unknown form of a rabies-related virus, he began feverishly trying to reach the couple by phone, wanting them to bring Chandler in to be placed under quarantine for observation. He was most likely less concerned with the animal's well-being and more interested in saving his practice and any future earnings, from the threatened lawsuit. But by then it was too late.

It was the results from the dog's tests that had pinged on the military's radar, causing them to begin their own, quiet investigation into the incident and to prepare for a worst-case scenario.

Brooks rubs her tired eyes because she hadn't slept in the last twenty-two hours since this shit-storm started, and the way things looked, she didn't expect to get any much-needed rest any time soon.

"Local agencies just aren't equipped to handle this number of animal attacks in such a short period of time," Riguez says, bringing Major Brooks back from her thoughts.

"Have the local authorities been able to capture any of the infected animals?" Brooks asks.

"At least one," Riguez answers.

"And...?" Brooks says, not wanting to start this bullshit again.

"That's where the reports start getting weird, Major. The first thing Animal Control did was take one of the dogs they managed to corner and muzzle to the closest vet for testing."

"Testing?"

"For rabies, Major. It's standard procedure in animal attacks. It was early in the event and the escalation in attacks hadn't been reported at that time," Riguez answers.

"Understood," Brooks says. "Continue."

"Apparently, the local vet took one look at the dog and decided to put it to sleep before starting the tests. This again is standard procedure for dangerous animals. The thing is, Major, the dog didn't go down. It didn't even yawn. They had the dog restrained on an exam table and shot it up three times."

"But the animal didn't die?"

"Just the opposite, Major. Reports indicate the animal appeared to become more aggressive with each injection. Eventually, the vet ordered the Animal Control officer who brought the dog in to shoot it."

"Seems like a reasonable decision," Brooks nods.

"Only that didn't work either," Riguez reports.

"What the fuck?" Brooks says, slipping out of her normal, disciplined composure.

"Not at first, anyway. The vet told the officer to avoid shooting the animal in the head so an accurate test for rabies could be performed, so he put the first bullet into the dog's chest."

"The first bullet?" Brooks asks, regaining her typical composure. "Any chance he missed with the first shot?"

"Not likely," Riguez answers. "He's a twenty-year veteran with Animal Control. He's had to put down seven animals in the field with his service piece during his career. I'm pretty sure he could hit a restrained dog from a few feet away."

"I see," Brooks says.

"The report is, the dog became enraged. Teeth snapping, convulsing, that sort of thing."

"Any chance the animal was just on autopilot, like when you cut the head off a chicken and it continues to flap around for a few more minutes?"

"I suppose it's possible, but not according to the report, Major. Apparently, the hellhound began struggling so violently, it started to slip out of the restrains in an attempt to get to the officer. The officer naturally panicked and fired three more, tightly grouped rounds into the dog."

"Is the animal dead or not?" Brooks asks, frustrated from feeling like she's still pulling the information out of her subordinated a single piece at a time.

"Yes, Major. But it took four bullets to the chest to do it."

"What caliber of gun was the officer firing? Standard issue?"

"Standard issue, nine-millimeter sidearm," Riguez replies with a nod.

"And we're certain it took four rounds to put the dog down?"

"That's what's being reported, Major. But we can't get one-hundred percent confirmation. The vet had the animal incinerated as a precaution after his examination."

"Have there been any human fatalities?"

"None reported yet. But this strain is so virulent, anyone bitten can be considered infected. Vaccination supplies for people are already running low and only seem to slow the progression of the infection. Human fatalities are an inevitable conclusion at this point."

"Anything else?" Brooks asks.

"One more thing," Riguez answers. "It's about the vet who started this whole mess.

"Dr. Faress," the Major nods.

"Apparently, after the news about the discovery of the Manchester's bodies made its way back to the good doctor, he sent an email to the CDC in Atlanta, offering his own speculation on the couple's demise and expressing his concerns about their missing dog."

"Goddamn it!" Brooks says. "How did they respond?"

"They didn't," Riguez says. "By that time, the doctor was already on our radar and we were monitoring all of his communications. Email, cell phone calls... everything. We intercepted the email before the CDC received it. But we won't be able to keep that up for much longer, especially after the shit hits the fan and more people become aware of the outbreak. There has already been a few news reports about the attacks from local television stations."

"Has anything been picked up by any of the national networks?"

"Not yet. But we've squashed several hundred reports on Twitter and other social media. It's all our tech guys can do to keep up and even then, some are slipping through. It's only a matter of time before this thing goes viral."

"Is that some kind of joke, Master Sergeant?" Brooks asks, instantly annoyed by her subordinate's last comment.

"No pun intended, Major," Riguez says, standing a little more rigid. "Just a poorly chosen phrase, but I think you get my point. Unless we do something pretty quickly, the internet is going to be flooded with reports. Some fact and some speculation, but there won't be a thing we can do to stop it once the levee breaks."

"Not unless we shut this shit down now," Brooks says.

"Do you mean the entire state of Ohio?" Riguez asks.

"To start with. The only thing we have going for us right now, is Lake Erie separating Ohio from Canada. If we don't get this contained soon, we could be talking about all the surrounding states as well. Michigan, Indiana, Kentucky, West Virginia, and Pennsylvania... maybe even New York."

"Ho-ly shit," Riguez gasps.

"You said it, Jorje. If things get bad, we might have to consider quarantining everything east of North Dakota, and down to Texas."

"That's half the country!" Riguez replies without thinking.

"I'm familiar with the map, Master Sergeant," Brooks replies.

"But my family lives in Chicago," Riguez says. "Can I at least call and warn them?"

"No way," Brooks replies sternly. "I need you here, monitoring the situation and reporting back to me. Is that clear?"

"Yes, Major," Riguez answers, snapping to attention and saluting his commanding officer.

"Then as you were," Brooks says, returning the salute and sending Riguez back to his duties. She watches him for a few seconds to make sure he's focused on the orders she's given before leaving. After the door closes behind her, she turns to the two security officers posted outside the communications room.

"Weinhardt," she begins, speaking directly to the larger of the two men. "I want you to go into the communication room and place Master Sergeant under house arrest. Confine him to his quarters until you hear from me. I want you to make sure he has no type of communication devices on him when you do. While he's doing that," she says, turning to the other officer. "I want you to tear his quarters apart and make sure he cannot contact any civilians. Then I want a detail posted outside his quarters and one soldier inside to keep an eye on him. Understood?"

"Yes ma'am," he replies.

"What's the Master Sergeant done?" Weinhardt asks.

"I'm trying to prevent what he's capable of doing," Brooks answers.

"What should I tell him if he asks what the charges are?"

"Tell him it's suspicion of sedition and potential treason. And if he resists, I want you to advise him you've been ordered to shoot him on the spot. No fucking around, no warning shots. If he doesn't cooperate, I want you to put a bullet in his head," she replies before considering Riguez's years of loyal service to her and the military. "But make sure he's clear about your intentions," she adds.

"Yes ma'am," Weinhardt replies with a salute.

"Carry on," Brooks replies, returning the gesture. "Report to me when you're done. I'll be in Colonel Beaurite's office."

Six minutes later, Brooks walked into Colonel Charles Beaurite's outer office. Corporal Lennox is seated at his desk and makes a half-hearted attempt to stand as the officer enters. They've gone through this same military ritual for the last eleven months. Normally, Brooks offers an *"as you were"* before Lennox can get up from the desk, but this morning is different. This morning, she stops and waits for the Corporal to stand and salute. To his credit, Lennox immediately realizes they're going *all-in* on the military protocol and stands to attention, delivering a textbook salute.

"Major," he says loud and clear, keeping his eyes forward.

"Is the Colonel available?" she asks, intentionally not returning the salute and keeping Lennox frozen in position.

"His calendar is clear for the next thirty-seven minutes," Lennox answers.

"Let him know I'm here," Brooks says, finally returning the salute, casually waving her hand somewhere near her right temple.

"Yes ma'am," Lennox replies. Without sitting, he touches the small earpiece with the built-in microphone he's wearing in his left ear, before speaking.

"Major Brooks is here to see you, sir," he says formally. "Yes, sir," he continues, his eyes darting to Brooks and then forward again. Lennox watches as Brooks tips her head slightly to the left, most likely wondering what the Colonel is saying. "Yes sir. Right away, sir," he says after receiving his orders. "The Colonel will see you now," Lennox says.

Slipping his hand under the edge of the desk, he pushes the button that releases the door lock to the Colonel's office from the outer office. A soft *buzz* emanates from the mechanism until

Brooks turns the heavy, brass handle on the door and Lennox releases the button. Brooks enters the large office but notices Lennox moving from behind his desk and leaving the outer office to enter the hallway as she closes the door behind her. Colonel Beaurite is sitting on the other side of his desk but rises to his feet when she enters. Not from a sense of military protocol, but because he was raised to always stand when a lady entered the room. He's a trim, six-foot-one and his hair is closely cropped with more than a little gray at the temples. He's in his late fifties but works out every day at the officer's gym and is easily in better shape than half of his younger officers. Occasionally, he still goes out with the enlisted men during their weekly, ten-mile morning run, just so everyone knows he can still keep up with his troops.

"You look tired, Carolyn. Please, have a seat," Colonel Beaurite says, forgoing any formality with his subordinate as he gestures to the chairs on the other side of his huge desk. The entire thing looked like it's been carved from a single tree and stained a dark brown. The top of the desk is covered from edge to edge with a thick layer of glass. Beneath the glass is a flat monitor screen, wired to the Colonel's secured-server computer with a touch keyboard built into the glass. As Brooks sits down in one of the two leather-covered chairs, Beaurite takes his again and taps the glass desktop, turning the monitor to the gray, privacy mode.

"I've sent Robert to get us some coffee. You look like you could use a cup," he says.

It takes Brooks a second to connect Lennox's first name to the man, before she replies, "Thank you, sir." While the Colonel can choose to waive military formality, Brooks is keenly aware that street only runs one way.

"When was the last time you slept?" he asks.

"What day is it, sir?"

"It's Saturday, Carolyn," he replies.

"Then it was Thursday, sir," Brooks replies.

Beaurite remains quiet for a moment, studying the dark circles forming under the Major's eyes and her rumpled uniform. If he'd been forced to guess from her appearance, he'd have said Wednesday. The Colonel clearly remembers when he held her rank, and before that. Soldiers routinely set personal health aside to perform their duty and he thinks about his past stretches of self-induced sleep deprivation as a younger man. He appreciates his current rank and the ability it affords him to get his standard, five to six hours of sleep each night. He has Brooks and his other officers to endure sleepless nights but knows if the orders came down to him from *on high*, he could easily be right there next to them. He considers how long it'll be before he's forced to order her to get some shuteye. Short of a total collapse, he knows it will take a direct order from him for Brooks to stand down. Of all his officers, she's easily the most stubborn and determined. He knows it has everything to do with showing everyone she's as competent and tough as the male officers. Given her shorter, physical stature, he's confident she's compensating for that as well.

"What do you have for me?" he asks, getting back to the business at hand. Before Brooks can answer, a soft chime comes from somewhere on the desk, followed by Lennox's voice, letting the Colonel know he's returned with their coffee.

"Bring it in know, please," Beaurite says. A few seconds later, the Corporal brings in a silver tray with a small, matching pot of coffee, two cups and the obligatory cream and sweeteners.

"There's also a few of the shortbread cookies you like," he tells the Colonel. "Would you like me to pour the coffee, sir?"

"Thank you, Robert. I think I can manage it. That'll be all for now," Beaurite says.

"Yes, sir," Lennox replies. "Your phone call with General Tibbitts is in thirty minutes," he reminds the camp's commander before leaving.

"Don't know how I managed without that kid," Beaurite says, as he gets up and heads over to the tray. "Best damn aid I've ever had," he adds, pouring coffee from the intricate, silver pot into the two delicate cups sitting on matching saucers. He sees Brooks watching him as he places a couple of the cookies with each cup and reads the nearly hidden expression on her face. "Rank has its privileges," he says, using the saucer to hand Brooks her cup of black coffee. Through the years, he knows this is how she prefers it, so he stopped bothering to offer cream and sugar years ago.

"Thank you, sir," she says, not replying to the Colonel's comment regarding the privileges of rank.

"Where were we?" he asks. They both know exactly where they were in their conversation before Lennox interrupted. But, Brooks also knows this is *the old man's* polite way of telling her to continue. She runs through the report Riguez had given her a few minutes ago, including the orders she gave to confine him to his quarters, and waits for Beaurite to process the information as she takes a sip of her coffee.

"It's probably for the best," Beaurite finally says with a heavy sigh. "Family is a powerful thing."

"Like they say, sir," she replies. "If the army wanted soldiers to have families, they'd have issued them one."

The Colonel's read through the file on Brooks, just like he has for all the soldiers under his command. He knows she grew up as an orphan, being shuttled from one foster home to the next. Never being able to stay in one place for very long. He knows she had several arrests for various misdemeanor crimes in her teens and how the psych tests the state had given her while in the foster care system showed she had a problem with authority and making emotional connections. Beaurite remembers reading this and thinking the military was a strange choice for the young rebel. But since she'd enlisted at eighteen, her record remained spotlessly dedicated to the service, with no indications or the slightest signs of insubordination.

"That's what they say," he says without betraying the thought Brooks might have gone a little too far but trusting in her judgment. "Be that as it may, I want you to personally check on him every few hours and start by explaining things to him."

"You want me to explain the reason for my orders, sir?" she asks.

"When this is all over, Carolyn, he's still going to be reporting to you. I don't want there to be any bad blood or hard feelings between the two of you. It's not good for morale."

"Yes, sir," Brooks answers, deciding instead to have Riguez transferred once this was all over. She'd of course wait the appropriate amount of time before she filed the orders and assure the Colonel it was at Riguez's request.

"Put our troops on alert," Beaurite tells her. "When I speak with General Tibbitts, I'll ask him to contact the Joint Chiefs and get them to call in support from the bases in the surrounding states. Notify the local National Guard we'll be calling on them for support. We're going to need to get moving on this if we're going to shut this cluster-fuck down."

"Do you think it's wise to invite the weekend warriors to the dance?" she asks.

The Colonel had always appreciated his Major's council as one of his lead officers, but he couldn't help noticing this was the second time in the same conversation she'd questioned his orders.

"I understand your concern, but it's a matter of numbers, Carolyn. If we're going to cover all the roads in and out of Ohio, we're going to need some more men. It's as simple as that. We'll make sure there aren't *Natty-Gs* operating on their own. They'll be matched up with military personnel in charge for every squad. The last thing we need is some local in a weekend uniform, letting his neighbors through our blockade because he's known them all his life and *trusts* them. Get everything in place here and we'll roll out in two hours."

"Where are we heading, sir?"

"In two hours, you'll be in the air with half our base's troops and touching down in Columbus thirty minutes later."

"Yes, sir. Colonel," Brooks says before standing and walking over to the small table. "You said, *I'll* be in the air with our troops. Will you be monitoring the situation from here at the base, sir?"

"I will," he replies. "I'm putting you in charge of this, Carolyn. I'll coordinate having military transport meet you and the troops on the tarmac. You'll be close to ground-zero, Carolyn. I want you to assess the situation and if needed, start *Operation Washout*. Once this shit-storm starts, there's no turning back and we can't afford any fuck ups. Understood?"

"Understood," she answers, setting her cup and saucer back on the tray. "One more thing if I may, sir."

"Speak freely," he says.

"I recommend we round up all the dogs on base and destroy them," Brooks says without hesitation.

The Colonel's surprised, and more than a little shocked, by Brooks' suggestion. He's always held the canine soldiers in high regard as fearless and loyal comrades in arms. Truth be told, he preferred them to many of his human troops. Rounding them up and killing them on base would be a hard blow to not only his but the entire camp's emotional well-being. But years of command keeps his expression carved in stone as he considers his trusted officer's recommendation and dismisses it. Still, he can't help wondering if Carolyn's always been this hardcore or if it's directly related to the situation they find themselves in now.

"I don't think that'll be necessary," he tells her.

"As you wish, sir," Brooks says before heading for the door. Beaurite places his fingertips on the button under the edge of his desk but hesitates when Brooks reaches for the handle. When she doesn't hear the familiar *buzz* from the lock, she turns to face him. "Is there something else, sir?"

"Just to be safe, have the canine soldiers gathered and have them quartered in the kennels for now. I want them monitored by video surveillance and I only want people in there to feed them. Be certain their human counterparts are assured this is purely a precautionary measure until the situation is resolved."

"Yes, sir," Brooks says before saluting and waiting for the lock to disengage. Outside the Colonel's office, she walks past Lennox without giving him a second glance or returning the salute he's been holding since he heard the buzzing of the door.

"I wonder what bug crawled up her ass?" the Corporal mutters to himself once he's certain the Major is out of hearing range.

CHAPTER FIVE

"I'm going to take a shower and wash the rest of this stuff off my hands," Pam says, looking at her stained hands as she and Dave walk into their apartment.

Helga, the receptionist, had blocked Pam from entering the clinic to clean up. She claimed she couldn't allow a potential biohazard into the clinic that wasn't an emergency situation. She was prepared to provide a copy of the corporate policy that covered this exact scenario if she was forced to. She was also quick to point out the sign in the window stating they had the right to refuse entrance to the premises. The police officers gave her a bottle of sterile water from their trunk so she could wash her hands off in the parking lot of the clinic. With a lack of soap, a single liter of water and a single, blue paper shop-towel, Pam's hands and forearms remained an awful shade of pink. It had, however, given her the opportunity to reassure herself she didn't have any cuts or scratches on her hands while she was doing her good deed and preventing the victim from bleeding to death.

"Yeah. You go ahead. I'll jump in after you're done," he replies. "I'm making a cup of coffee. Do you want one?"

"What?" Pam yells from their bedroom. "I can't fucking hear you!"

"I said, I'm going to make some fucking coffee. Do you want some?" Dave shouts from the bedroom door but not bothering to step inside the room.

"Yes, please," Pam replies at a normal volume and as sweet as she can be.

"Yeah," Dave mutters, hearing their bathroom door close. "Now you're all nice and shit when I'm offering coffee."

"What did you say?" Pam shouts from the bathroom as she turns on the water, making any chance of Dave being able to respond without going into the bathroom, impossible.

He decides to feign ignorance, and if Pam presses the issue after her shower, he'll swear he never heard her. He rationalizes this, because he knows from experience, providing effortless coffee is an amazing way to wipe someone's memory. He preps a couple mugs with cream and sugar before popping the first coffee cartridge into the *Keurig* and pressing the button for *large*. He waits the fifty seconds it takes for the machine to finish brewing before it starts spitting air and beginning its refilling act. He repeats the process with the other mug before stirring them both. Dave considers making Pam toast too but decides the coffee's enough to atone for his crime and heal his bruised karma. It's not like he'd killed anyone. Carrying the mugs into the bedroom, he enters in time to see his wife exiting the bathroom wrapped in a towel.

"See anything you like?" she asks, letting the towel fall to the floor and holding out one hand to Dave.

"Yes, I do," he answers with a sly grin, setting the steaming cups on top of the dresser.

"You're gross and need a shower! I want the coffee," Pam says, her outstretched hand making the *give it here* gesture.

"Tease," he replies, handing her one of the mugs.

"Maybe after you've showered, *Captain Quint* can come out

and do some *deep-C diving*," she says with a wink.

"*Farewell and adieu to you, fair Spanish ladies. Farwell and adieu, to you ladies of Spain,*" Dave begins to sing as he walks into the bathroom and turns on the water.

"Get in the goddamn shower," Pam laughs, throwing her wet towel at his back.

"*For we've received orders for to sail back to Boston. And so nevermore shall we see you again,*" he croons, dropping his pants to the floor.

"Clean up, and thanks for the coffee," she says.

"*Show me the way to go home,*" Dave sings, shaking his naked hips at her as he continues his rendition of the best scene from one of his all-time, favorite movies.

"I think we're going to need a bigger boat," Pam smirks, quoting from the same movie.

"*I'm tired and I want to go to bed,*" he continues undaunted. "*I had a little drink about an hour ago, and it's got right to my head.*"

"Pump it out, chief," Pam says, reaching for the doorknob as the bathroom begins filling with steam from the shower.

"Hey," Dave replies, pausing his lyrical recitation. "I thought I was Quint!"

"Stop playing with yourself, Hooper," she quotes, pulling the door shut.

"I don't have to take this abuse much longer!" he shouts at the door, getting in the last movie line as he steps into the shower. He's no sooner pulled the curtain closed when Pam bursts through the door.

"So, eleven hundred men went into the water, three hundred sixteen men came out, and the sharks took the rest, June 29th, 1945," she says in a deadpan voice.

"Asshole," Dave chuckles. "You couldn't just let me have it."

"Thanks again for the coffee," she replies, blowing over the lip of her mug before taking a sip. She nearly dribbles it down her chin from the smirk still on her face before leaving.

After his shower, Dave dries off and dresses in clean jeans and an *Obey Cthulhu* t-shirt, printed to look like the *Coca-Cola* logo. He stuffs the Zippo lighter and pocket knife he always carries into his left pocket and his disposable lighter into his right. When it's fueled, his Zippo is the best lighter he's ever owned, but he hates it when it's empty and he can't light a smoke. He grabs his cell phone, still plugged in from the night before. Dave sees the green light flashing in the upper corner of the dark screen, letting him know he's gotten a message. Tapping the display to bring it to life, he has just enough time to see he's missed a call, when Weird Al Yankovic's, *"White & Nerdy"* comes blaring from the phone's tiny speaker. He taps the green button on the screen, accepting the call from his eldest son before saying into the phone, "Hey, Zack!"

Pam and Dave have four children between them, from previous marriages. Amy, the oldest of the four lives in Seattle with her husband, Travis and their daughter, Alexandria. Everyone in the family calls her Ally or just plain Al. Zack's the younger of Dave's two, biological children. He and his wife, Brigette, live a hundred and fifty miles north, outside of Akron with her two young sons, Braxton and Jaxon. Pam's oldest son Joe lives in Columbus with his friend, Dakota and Joe's hyperactive dog, Bongo. Ben lives alone in his own apartment five minutes away from Zack by car. Twelve minutes if he's riding a bicycle, which Ben does often to visit his brother. While the kids all call their non-biological parents by their first names, they always refer to each other as brother and sister, with *step* never being a consideration to any of them. The four range in age from Amy at thirty-four, to Ben at a fresh twenty-one. Although they come from different relationships, Pam and Dave have always considered them all *their* kids, doing their best to treat them all equally. This hasn't always been easy for the couple and has been the subject of more than one, heated discussion over their seventeen-year marriage. There are two years between each biological sibling with a seven-year gap in the middle of the sets. It's hard to believe the difference in the parenting skills needed with that kind of span.

"Why didn't you answer your phone?" Zack asks without saying hello.

"I must've been in the shower when you called. What's up?" Dave asks, picking up on the urgent tone in Zack's voice.

"Are you watching the news?"

"You know better than that, son. What's going on?" Dave replies, hearing something more than urgency in his son's words.

"Right. The fucking cable thing," Zack says. "You need to listen to the news. Get to a television that has it or turn on the radio. You have one of those, right?"

"Our alarm clock still has one, but the last time I tried using it, the reception was for shit."

"But, you still have the internet!"

"Just tell me what's going on. Are you alright?"

"No, Dad. I'm not alright," Zack answers, his voice cracking. "I just had to kill our dog with a shovel."

"Señor Gherkins? What the hell for?" Dave asks as a black-hole starts forming in the pit of his stomach.

"Who's on the phone?" Pam asks, seeing it pressed to his ear as she steps into their bedroom. It wasn't like this was the first time she found him having a verbal exchange with himself, but she'd thought she'd check to make sure.

"It's Zack," he tells her. "I think he just killed his dog."

"Señor Gherkins?" she replies.

"I had to kill him," Zack tells his father.

"With a shovel?" Dave asks.

"With a what?" Pam asks, her brows furrowing.

"Yeah, Dad. A shovel," Zack answers.

"I'm trying to find out," Dave tells Pam. "Let me put you on speaker," he says to Zack. Moving the phone away from his face, he taps the icon to set it to speakerphone. "Now, what the fuck happened?" he asks, talking to the screen.

"We're at home and I was watching the stuff happening down there on the news. So, I was getting ready to call and check on you and Pam. That's when I realized one of the boys put the dog in the backyard. So, I went to check on him and Señor Gherkins was like, acting bat-shit crazy. All, foaming at the mouth and stuff."

"Jesus Christ!" Dave says, looking at Pam as they instantly recalled the events from this morning.

"The second my foot hit the grass, he came at me," their son continued. "He was snarling and trying to bite me. Like he didn't even recognize me. Just like the reports are saying about the going on down there. I started looking for anything I could find to defend myself. That's when I grabbed the shovel and hit him with it."

"But it didn't stop him, did it?" David asks, thinking about the dog that had attacked the woman this morning.

"The fuck it didn't!" Zack replies. "I've seen the news stories and looked on the internet. I wasn't taking any chances by trying to just hurt him. I smashed his skull with the damn shovel! Then I planted the blade in the back of his neck and jumped on the fucking thing," he says with a noticeable sob. "Dad... I cut Señor Gherkins' head off with a fucking shovel!"

"What reports are you talking about?" Dave asks, fearing the worst. Zack fills his parents in on current events, causing Pam to grab her cell phone and start searching the web.

"I don't see anything from the national news channels," Pam says after a few minutes. "But, the internet is starting to go apeshit. Wait... The local Fox News station might have reported something about it, but whatever it is, they're trying to blame it on Obama."

"They're fucking idiots," Dave replies. "Are you guys all okay?" he asks Zack.

"We're safe," Zack answers. "I've barricaded the doors and windows."

"From dogs?" Dave asks.

"Dad! They're saying the people who've been bitten are starting to react like the animals did! Going all crazy and attacking people. The one post I saw said some people had to be killed!"

"I just read that one," Pam says with a dire expression.

"Like a zombie?" Dave asks them both.

"No," Pam replies. "But the post says it took four rounds from a twelve-gauge to put one of the people down."

"Right," Zack agrees. "I'm not screwing around. I'm going right for the head if I have to. I tried calling Ben after I couldn't get ahold of you the first time, but the little fucker never answers his damn phone!"

"Did you try texting him?" Pam asks into the phone.

"Why can't he just answer the fucking call?" Zack asks her.

"Joe doesn't either," Pam says, like that explains everything.

"I know!" Zack replies. "I tried him after Ben! What the hell is wrong with those two?"

"Nothing," Pam says as another siren starts up somewhere outside, in the distance. "They just prefer texting."

"Amy and I answer our phones," he protests.

"Amy does," Pam replies, making the unspoken comment that Zack often misses his calls and ignores text messages.

"Stop!" Dave says loudly, interrupting the debate they've all had before.

"What?" Zack says before his father can continue. "Shit! Brigette says she just read one where they say they're going to call in the National Guard to take control of the situation. They're talking about sealing off Ohio, Dad!"

"Listen to me," Dave says, taking control. "Do you guys still have your guns?"

"We sold mine but Brigette still has hers," Zack answers.

"Fine. Get the gun and all the bullets you have in the house. Put as much food and water you can safely get into your car, making sure to leave room for the boys," Dave says. "Then I want you to start driving west. We need to get out before the military takes over."

"If, the military takes over," Pam says, having seen her fair share of hoaxes on the internet.

"When they take control," Dave replies, knowing deep down, this isn't a hoax. Some of the reports might be exaggerated, but something was going horribly awry and he doesn't want to take any chances.

"I think our car is on *E*," Zack says.

"Then get some fucking gas!" Dave replies, feeling forced to state the obvious. "I want you and Brigette to keep trying to get ahold of Ben. Try texting him," he adds, diffusing any arguments before they can start again. "When you reach him, tell him to call me. I want you guys to take the fastest route out of state, probably 224. Then angle north to I-90. We'll meet up with you in Indiana late this afternoon or tonight. We'll plan on just outside of Gary and avoid Chicago if we can."

"What are you guys going to do?" Zack asks.

"The first thing I'm doing is calling your sister and letting her know we're all probably headed her way, while Pam contacts Joe. Then we're going to pack up whatever we can grab and head out," Dave answers. "I'll plan on taking 70 West, since it's the shortest route, but if that's fucked, we may be forced to head south first, and then cut through Cincinnati, maybe the edge of Kentucky before turning north. If that happens, we'll meet up closer to Davenport, so watch for a call from us. In the meantime, let me know if you guys *do* or *don't* contact Ben. Got it?"

"Got it, Dad. We'll see you all tonight," Zack replies, sounding more focused than he had when their conversation started.

"And Zack!" Dave says before his son can hang up on their call.

"Yeah Dad..."

"Be extra careful. Avoid other people as much as you can. If you can't do that and still get gas in your car, then fucking steal one. But, no matter what happens, keep your family safe."

"We love you guys," Pam adds.

"We love you guys, too and we'll talk soon," Zack says right before he ends the call.

"Do you think things are as bad as they sound?" Pam asks Dave after a second of them both staring at the phone.

"Start texting Joe. I'm calling Amy, he says in way of an answer as he scrolls to the contact list on his phone and taps their daughter's picture.

"Good morning!" Amy says, cheerfully answering her phone on the third ring. "I was just getting ready to call you."

"Amy! Don't talk and just listen to me. We have an uppercase situation," Dave begins, setting the parameters for their conversation.

"Go ahead," Amy replies, her tone becoming serious based on her father's use of a term he only used for the most fucked up situations.

"I don't have time to explain, and don't ask me if I've been drinking. I haven't started yet, and that's not the reason I'm calling. I need you to go outside and kill your dogs," he tells her, referring to both large dogs her family has had since Ally was little. "Go ahead, I'll wait," he adds.

"Trav!" Amy yells to her husband who's somewhere else in their house. "Take Al to her room. Dad says I have to kill Frankie and SoCo."

"He wants you to what?" Dave hears Travis reply.

"He said I need to go shoot the dogs right now!" she repeats.

"You remember your dad drinks, a lot, right?" Travis asks.

"I know that, but he said we're in an uppercase situation."

"Oh shit! Come on Al!" Travis calls to their daughter. "Let's go play in your room. Mom's going outside."

"What's she doing out there?" he hears his granddaughter

ask as Amy sets down the phone and gets her pistol from the gun safe in her and Travis's bedroom. Less than a minute later, Dave hears four muffled shots being fired.

"This is why she's my fucking favorite!" Dave says to Pam as he retrieves the pistol-grip shotgun he's owned since before they were married, from under the bed. "She didn't even question me on this!"

"She's a good daughter," Pam agrees, tapping *Send* to the message she's sending Joe.

"Do you want to tell me now why I just shot your granddaughter's dogs?" Amy asks a moment later, sounding a little out of breath.

"What?" Dave asks, fumbling with the phone as he plugs six of the dozen shells he owns, into the tube of his twelve-gauge.

"Goddamn it, Dad!" Amy shouts into the phone. "You *have* been drinking!"

"No, I haven't, and I don't have time to explain everything because we're still trying to get in touch with Joe and Ben."

"They never answer their phones," Amy interrupts. "Did you try texting them? That's what I do."

"I'm in fucking hell," Dave sighs before continuing. "Just listen to me. Check the internet for what's going on out here and catch up. Then go and buy as much food as you can store in your house. Make sure and get enough to feed all of us for at least a week or two."

"All of us?" Amy asks. "Are you and Pam coming out to Seattle?"

"More than likely. And we're bringing the rest of the family with us, if we can."

CHAPTER SIX

From the phone of Joe Brannon...

Mom – 10:02AM
Joe! Are you there?

Mom – 10:05AM
Call me as soon as you get this!

Mom – 10:10AM
Call me!

Mom – 10:12AM
Goddamn it Joe! Ducking call me!

Mom – 10:12AM
*Fucking

Mom – 10:17AM
You're making me worry about you. Call me as soon as you see this!

Mom – 10:20AM
Call me!!!!!!

Mom – 10:26AM
If you don't call me in 5 minutes I'm coming over!

Mom – 10:38AM
Ducking call me!!!!!

Mom – 10:38AM
Ducking auto-correct!

Mom – 10:38AM
*Fucking!!!! Call me! This is an emergency!!!!!!!!

Mom – 10:47AM
We're coming over in 10 minutes

Mom – 11:00AM
Where the duck are you????

Mom – 11:00AM
*fuck

Mom – 11:12AM
We're coming over. You better ducking be there!

Mom – 11:12AM
Goddamn it…

Mom – 11:14AM
I'm SERIOUS. CALL ME! DAVE'S GETTING PISSED

Mom – 11:17AM
It's been over an hour and you're still not answering??? Where the hell are you?

Mom – 11:21AM
Duck it! We're leaving now. We'll be there in 20.

Mom – 11:21AM
*Fuck it

Me – 11:39AM
Hey mom

Mom – 11:39AM
Where are you?

Me – 11:41AM
What do I need to make tot casserole?

Mom – 11:41AM
Where are you!!!!????

Me – 11:44AM
At home I know I need burger and tots but I can't remember the rest

Mom – 11:44AM
WTF Joe!!!!!

Me – 11:45AM
What kind of soup do I need Chicken or celery

Mom – 11:45AM
It doesn't ducking matter!

Mom – 11:45AM
*fucking

Mom – 11:46AM
Parking now. Go to your door but don't open the trucker until we get there!

Mom – 11:46AM
*fucker

Me – 11:46AM
Did you bring the soup?

Mom – 11:47AM
No

Me – 11:47AM
K ☹

CHAPTER SEVEN

Dave eases their Rogue into the nearly empty parking lot of Joe's apartment. There are only a few cars in the lot so he's able to grab one of the three closest spots to Joe's door and quickly turns the engine off. Keeping the doors locked, they wait, scanning the parking lot for any signs of movement. Their attention is immediately drawn to a plastic grocery bag drifting away from the apartment garbage dumpster, moving like a slow-motion tumbleweed across the empty stalls.

During the drive over, they'd seen at least three packs of dogs roaming the streets and dozens of people on foot, trying to avoid them. There was more than one person they saw, limping along the streets with a blood-coated leg or arm and pale complexions. The first one was in the park, just a block from their apartment. He looked like he might have been a mid to late twenty-something, but it was hard to tell. They saw him slowly walking in a large circle on the grass, his arms held out slightly from his sides. His eyes looked sunken and dazed like he was going into deep shock. At first, they slowed to a near stop, planning to help him, or at least take him someplace safe. That was until the guy completed more of his loop, and his rear came into view. The entire back of his jogging outfit was covered in sticky crimson, caused by whatever had ravaged the flesh at the base of his neck. As he came farther along his arc, they saw the remains of the broken leash, still dangling from his right wrist. The guy turned his head their direction and his blood-filmed eyes locked onto Pam. He started stumbling straight toward them in an awkward shuffle. It was then, they could see the streams of mucus flowing from his nose. His lips are pulled back in a snarl as foam dripped from his mouth.

"Just go!" Pam had shouted as Dave was already easing his foot down onto the accelerator pedal.

The man compensated, obviously more limber than he'd first appeared, because he started running at them with a more controlled stride. He was rapidly closing the distance, so Dave pressed harder on the gas. The man adjusted again, changing from his straight-line approach to an intercept course, and shifting gears into an all-out sprint.

"The son of a bitch was playing opossum!" Dave shouted, stomping on the pedal. An instant later, a short scream escaped Pam when the guy slammed against the rear portion of their car. The vehicle rocked from the impact. The human-shaped creature had just enough time to howl in frustration and bash his fist against the rear door window before being spun onto his ass behind them. Dave glanced in the rearview mirror as a chill went down his spine. In that moment, Dave knew if he'd waited any longer to hit the gas, the monster would have crashed into Pam's door, and from the speed he was moving, he'd have come through her window. His mind played the scene out in his head. The thing smashing through the safety glass, gore-covered teeth tearing into Pam's throat, her blood spraying onto the inside of the windshield. Dave shook his head to dislodge the vision and refocused on the road.

"We can't stop to help anyone," he'd told Pam as he reached

for her hand and squeezed it, reassuring himself she was still alive. "It's too risky."

"No way," she'd agreed, and squeezed his hand in return.

The other run-in they had during the drive was from a rabid Schnauzer. The beast had tried to intimidate them into stopping their car by standing in the road and baring its teeth. Dave avoided the confrontation by dispatching the canine with the front tires and a satisfying *thump*.

"Do you see anything?" Pam asks Dave as they continue searching the parking lot for any signs of a threat.

"The grocery bag almost made me piss myself," Dave confesses as he stares out through the windshield.

"My brave hero," Pam says.

"Pissing myself might have been an exaggeration, but it *did* startle me, a little."

"Uh-huh," Pam replies.

"Okay. I don't see anyone," Dave says a moment later. "Do you see Joe?"

"No. But, I told him not to open the door until we got to it," she reminds him.

"Have you tried texting him again?"

"Not after the frowny face," Pam says.

"Right. The fucking tot casserole recipe again. We've given it to him over a half-dozen times," Dave says.

"I know."

"I mean, all he has to do is scroll back on your message thread to get it!"

"I know. But maybe he deletes his messages after he gets them," Pam replies.

"Oh, give me a break!" he says, turning to reach into the

back seat.

"He might. You don't know!"

"I know he's fucking lazy," Dave says, pulling the short, pistol-grip shotgun from the back. He sets it on his lap, pointing the business end toward his door instead of at Pam.

"He has a full-time job and a part-time one, and he takes a few classes at night. He's not lazy!" Pam says.

"I know he's not! But he's just..." Dave says, pausing to take a deep breath. "Look. I'm just a little worked up right now with everything and I may be overreacting a little. All I want to do is get Joe..."

"And Dakota," Pam interrupts.

"And Dakota," Dave nods. "Then I want to know Zack has Ben and for all of us to be a few hundred miles west of Ohio by dark." Looking at his wristwatch, he sees it's almost noon and knows it will be dark in less than five hours.

"Okay," he continues. "Joe's door is about thirty yards from us."

"More like a hundred feet," Pam says.

"What, the fuck, ever," he replies.

"I'm just saying, I think it's more than thirty yards!"

"By ten feet, maybe! What difference does it make?"

"About four steps, and remember the guy from the park," Pam replies.

"Good point," Dave says, checking the safety on the shotgun before continuing. "It's a hundred feet to Joe's door. We can cover that in a few seconds, but we do not run unless we see someone."

"Or something," Pam adds.

"Or something," he agrees. "Are you ready?"

"Wait until I close my door before you open yours. By that time, I'll be coming around the back of the car and we'll move together. But make sure and stay behind me!" Dave says, pushing the gun's safety button to the *off* position and reaching for his door handle.

"On three," he says. "One... Two... Three," he almost shouts before bouncing his head off the inside of the window and slamming his shoulder into the door.

"It's still locked," Pam reminds him as he rubs the side of his head.

"Yeah. Thanks," Dave replies before pushing the button on the armrest that controls the door locks. "On three," he says again.

"Just go," Pam tells him.

"You don't want a countdown?"

"I've already had one and they're not as cool as I'd hoped. Just go and I'll follow once you're around the car."

"Good plan," Dave says, pulling on the handle and feeling the door unlatch.

Without another word, Dave slips out of their vehicle and quietly closes his door. He moves around the back of the car, the shotgun tracking left and right for any threatening targets. When he gets to the other side, Pam is already out and waiting for him. He gives her a nod to tell her to start moving, right before she swings the door closed, he knows he's too late to stop her. In the quiet of the parking lot, the car door sounds like a cannon going off when it makes contact with the frame, his fingers clenching the grip of the twelve-gauge as the door latches.

"Go!" Dave whispers urgently.

"Sorry," Pam whispers back, her expression showing real regret.

"It's okay. Just go!" he tells her.

They move quickly, their eyes constantly scanning the parking lot and the connecting street. Dave keeps the gun moving in unison with his line of sight. Wherever he looks, the barrel points that way. He makes certain to keep Pam behind him and out of his field of fire, should the need present itself. They make it to Joe's door in less than thirty seconds, to find it's locked.

"Where is he?" Dave whispers, trying the knob a second time.

"I told him to wait at the door," Pam replies.

Dave quietly knocks on the door to let Joe know they're outside, but there's no answer. He knocks harder and listens again.

"Be right there!" Joe shouts from somewhere in the apartment.

"You gotta be fucking kidding me!" Dave hisses, turning to face the parking lot with the gun while they wait for Joe to open the door. He hears the lock being turned from the inside and presses his back to Pam's, keeping himself between her and the lot.

"Hi Mom. Hi Dave," Joe says in a cheerful tone.

He turns without ever actually making eye contact with his parents. His thoughts temporarily preoccupied as he turns to head back down the short entry hall leading to his living room. Pam follows him in, and Dave backs up through the open door, quickly closing and locking it behind them.

"Where's Dakota?" Pam asks Joe.

"He's in the shower," he replies as Dave enters the living

room.

Dave stops and takes a deep breath when he sees Joe is safe but becomes instantly angry when he takes a second look. Standing in his living room, Joe is holding the cordless game controller to his Xbox version *what-the-fuck-ever* in one hand, and his cell phone in the other as he scrolls through something with his thumb.

"Sorry I missed your phone calls," Joe says to his mother, finally looking up from his phone with a puzzled expression. "What's with the shotgun, Dave?" he asks.

Instead of answering his son, Dave marches across the living room and slaps the electronic devices from Joe's hands, sending them clattering to the carpeted floor.

"Hey! Asshole!" Joe shouts.

"What the fuck is wrong with you?" Dave shouts over him.

"The same thing that was wrong with us, two hours ago, before we knew anything was wrong! He was busy living his life!" Pam adds, glaring first at Dave and then Joe, before continuing in a low growl. "Now, everyone, stop fighting, and keep, your fucking, voices down!"

"Sorry, Mom," Joe says quietly, as he and Dave look down at their feet.

"She's *your* mother," Dave whispers to him.

"You married her," he replies.

"Hey, Mr. and Mrs. Richter," Dakota says, coming down the stairs that lead to the two bedrooms and second bathroom upstairs. He must've heard the shouting because he hasn't bothered to fully dress after his shower. He's wearing a thick, terrycloth robe and still has a towel wrapped around his neck, using one end to dry his wet hair.

"I told you, you could call me Mom," Pam tells him in the same, low tone she used with Dave and Joe.

Feeling the waves of tension in the room, he comes to a stop on the bottom step. "Right," Dakota replies, easing down the last step to the apartment-sized living room. "Hi, Mom. Hi..."

"Dave," he fills in for him with a nod.

"Yeah. Hi Dave," Dakota says. His eyes are drawn to the shotgun in Dave's hands, so he avoids any sudden movements and speaks slowly. "If we'd known you guys were planning on coming over, we'd have cleaned up a little more and made snacks."

"If you'd known we were coming over?" Pam hisses, glaring at Joe again.

"Am I, missing something?" Dakota asks, realizing he's started off by saying the wrong thing.

"Let's try this again," Dave says. "Do you two know what's going on?"

"Not a clue. I just heard the shouting and came down," he replies, his eyes still focused on the twelve-gauge.

"Oh! Shit," Dave says, realizing he's aiming the gun at Dakota before lowering the barrel to point at the floor.

"Thanks," Dakota says, visibly relaxing.

"I meant, out there," Dave says, gesturing back toward the front door.

"Same answer. Not a clue," Joe says. "I just bought the new, *Dead Army* video game and we've been playing it since last night."

"You mean, *Ghost Team's Reckoning*! How is it?" Dave asks.

"It's super cool," Joe says. "Like I said, we've been playing since last night and we're only through like, the third campaign.

I think there's supposed to be ten and the graphics are incredible! Wanna see?" he asks, leaning down to retrieve the controller and his phone from the floor.

"Maybe some other time," Pam interrupts before her husband can get sucked in. She enjoys a good, survival-horror game more than most, but now's probably not the time for Dave to start a long-term commitment with a game console. "You both need to sit down while we fill you in," she says, speaking to Joe and Dakota.

"So, is that what all the sirens have been about?" Dakota asks after the couple finished with their rundown of events. "I thought it was just, you know, a home game weekend."

"What are we doing?" Joe asks.

"To start, Dakota should probably get dressed," Pam answers.

"Then you guys are going to grab some of your stuff and we're getting out of here," Dave says.

"Where are we going?" Joe asks.

"We're meeting up with your brothers once we're out of Ohio, and we're all going to Amy's," Dave replies. "Pam, try to call Zack and see if they have Ben with them while I help the boys get their shit together."

Ten minutes later, Joe, Dave, and Pam are standing at the front door. Joe's carrying two small duffle bags filled with the things he and Dakota gathered together.

"Zack and Brigette aren't answering their phones," Pam tells Dave after her fifth attempt. "Do you think something's happened?"

"Either that, or they're just our children," he replies.

"Did you try texting them?" Joe asks.

"Stop it," Dave says. "Where's Dakota?"

"He's grabbing Bongo from upstairs."

"The dog can't come with us," Dave says firmly.

"Well, we're not leaving him. He'll starve," Joe replies.

"Better than him taking a bite out of any of us when he gets peakish," Dave tells him.

"I'm not leaving Bongo," Joe says.

"He can't come. What if he's infected and goes all *Cujo* in the car?" Dave asks.

"He won't," Joe says.

"You don't know that!" Dave counters. "He stays!"

"Then so do I," Joe replies, dropping the duffel bags in the entryway.

"Don't be stupid!"

"We're ready," Dakota announces as he comes down the stairs, carrying the squirming time bomb in his arms. The dog's tail starts beating against Dakota's ribs like it's trying to break the bones when he sees Pam and Dave.

"Take him back upstairs and lock him in a room!" Dave demands as he fingers the safety button the twelve-gauge.

"Why?" Dakota asks as Bongo wriggles free, leaps to the floor and makes a beeline for Pam.

"Goddamn it!" Dave says, frantically clicking the safety off and leveling the barrel of the twelve-gauge on the dog. A few feet before the furry demon gets to Pam, Dave pulls the trigger, trying to cut the dog in half before it can sink its infected teeth into his wife.

"Don't!" Joe yells, drowning out the disappointing click from the guns firing pin hitting dead space that only Dave hears.

"Get back!" Dave bellows to Pam as he pumps a round into

the chamber and takes aim.

"Wait!" Joe shouts, stepping into Dave's line of fire as the dog leaps.

"Move!" Dave demands.

"David!" Pam yells.

"Move, goddamn it!" he tells Joe again.

"David! Don't shoot!" Pam says, vigorously petting an apparently uninfected Bongo.

"I told you so," Joe says, moving out of the way so Dave can see the dog only attacking Pam with a wagging tail and whimpers of elation. Dave stares, seeing the dog release a few drops of urine onto the carpet from its excitement.

"Do you want to stop pointing that thing at me?" Pam asks as she scratches behind Bongo's ears with both hands. "Who's a good boy?" she coos to the dog as its butt wriggles back and forth. Dave quickly points the barrel at the ceiling and pushes the safety button back into place.

"Jerk," Joe mutters, moving over to his mother to lavish some affection on the dog Dave was preparing to shoot.

"Fine," Dave concedes. "He might not be infected now, but he's still not coming with us. The reports say dogs have turned on the owners all over the state. We can't take the chance."

"He's obviously a threat," Pam says, getting in one last pet before Bongo escapes her ministrations and runs to Dave. The happy fur-ball rubs against his legs before jumping up and setting its front paws on Dave's thighs, begging for his attention.

"Stop it," Dave says without much force as he moves his leg.

"He doesn't look infected," Pam says with a smirk.

"That doesn't mean he won't be," Dave replies. He takes another step back and separates himself from the dog. Realizing

Dave's not playing along, Bongo returns to Pam for more cuddles.

"But he's not now," Joe says. "And if he does get infected, or whatever, I'll put him down myself."

"And if he doesn't, I will," Dakota adds.

"It looks like you're outvoted, three to one," Pam says.

"I'm not sure when this became a fucking democracy," Dave says, finally lowering the shotgun to point it at the floor, looking from Joe to Dakota. "Fine. He's your responsibility. But if he goes crazy and anything happens to Pam, I'm holding you both responsible."

"Why not me?" she asks.

"Because if that happens, I'm the one that's going to have to put *you* down and I'm not taking the karmic hit for that," he tells her. "That's going to be on these two and I'll never forgive them."

There's a moment of silence between the four of them, acknowledging the gravity of what Dave's said. Bongo yips, breaking the tension for everyone but Dave, who's grip tightens on the gun for a second before he speaks.

"Joe, grab your bags. Dakota, get the dog and carry him to the car. I don't want us to have to chase the damn thing when he decides to sniff around your neighbor's flower beds. Pam and I will be in front and I want the two of you to stay close behind us until we get to our car."

"We can take my car too," Joe says.

"No. I want us all in one vehicle and ours is already packed. When we get to *our* car, we'll open the back doors for you before we get in. Don't screw around. Just get in and lock your doors," Dave tells them before looking through the peephole in the front door. "I don't see anything out there but that doesn't mean shit. There could be an entire pack of dogs sitting quietly on the other side of the door waiting for us to deliver lunch."

"So, now what?" Pam asks quietly.

"We go anyway," he tells her, bring the shotgun to the ready position and clicking off the safety. "I want you to open the door for me but then step back and don't crowd me. If anything's hiding on the other side, I'm going to shoot first and then slam the door shut. Got it?" The three of them nod. "Okay. On three," he says, taking a deep breath and curling his finger over the trigger and aiming the gun toward the bottom of the door.

"Wait," Pam whispers. "On three? Or one, two—"

"Just open the door," Dave interrupts.

"Right," Pam says, pulling the door open.

Dave sweeps the barrel across the opening. He keeps it low at first, making sure there's nothing preparing to chew off his legs. Stepping into the doorway. He quickly pans right and then left, clearing the outside of the door. He moves the gun up, keeping it aligned with his eyes as he checks the parking lot.

"It looks clear," he says, focusing his attention to the area around their car and heading for it.

The four make their way from the door to the car like circus clowns. Not quite stumbling their way across the lot, but also not managing to keep out of each other's way. Getting to the rear door on his side of the car, Dave takes one hand from the gun to pull the door handle, but nothing happens. He stares through both car windows, watching Pam fumble for the keys he'd given her when they got out of the car. He'd done this in case anything happened to him so she'd still have an avenue of escape. He hadn't noticed she'd locked it when they exited but apparently, she had.

"Sorry," she mouths, looking back at him through the side windows as she pushes the button on the remote fob. The parking lights flash twice, and the door locks slide open. Dave and Pam pull the doors open for Joe, Dakota, and a squirming Bongo before jerking open theirs and getting in. The timing is perfect and they all slam their doors at the same time, loud enough to make the sound echo off the facing apartments.

"Shit!" Dave says. Pam hands him the keys and it takes two stabs for him to get them into the ignition and get the car started.

Glancing in the back, Joe sees all the dried and packaged food his parents packed from their home, including two cases of bottled water. There's a cooler Joe assumes is filled with things from their freezer and a few bags and boxes with dry goods, bread, fruit, and a box of microwave popcorn.

"Jesus! Did you leave anything behind?" he asks Pam.

"Not much," she answers.

"How about a can opener?" he asks, spotting the two large boxes, full of an assortment of canned foods.

"Fuck..." Dave says, looking at Pam.

"I grabbed one," she assures him.

"Thanks honey. Did you get ahold of Zack?"

"No. I'll try again once we get on the road," she tells Dave. At the same moment, two people come shuffling from one of the apartments, their bloody-muzzled Pitbull scrambling out in front of them.

"What about Gramma and Grampa?" Joe asks as Dave drops the car into gear.

"Shit!" Pam gasps. Not from the presence of the shamblers,

but because of her son's question. She and Dave had been so fixated on their kids, she hadn't even thought about her own parents' safety. Dave's parents were divorced, but they'd both passed away within eight months of each other, shortly after she and Dave were married. Her parents are both still alive and living in Canton, about thirty minutes south of Akron, where Zack and Ben lived. Just the two of them in their early seventies, and their eighty-pound Golden Retriever, Apollo.

Apollo has always been a great, loving dog. Mike and Lynn got him from a rescue a few years ago. He'd been a service dog for an elderly woman but when she finally passed, her drunk, asshole husband took it out on Apollo. This treatment ruined him from ever being a service animal again, but the couple fell in love with him at first sight. He was always happily bringing them things as they sipped their coffee in the mornings. Sometimes it was the newspaper or his leash. Other times it was a random shoe, an article of clothing from the laundry hamper or something he'd snuck inside from one of his walks and hidden in the home to proudly present to his owners at a later date. And if he wasn't bringing you one of his treasures, he was showing you something he found fascinating. Apollo would do this by gently taking your hand or wrist in his mouth, holding it between his large canine teeth, and leading you to it.

"Try the boys again. Then call your folks," Dave tells her, hurrying out of the parking lot as the two figures start running for them.

CHAPTER EIGHT

"Any new reports?" Brooks asks Riguez's replacement. The Major was on her way to the airfield for the sync-up with her troops but wanted the latest intel on the situation before leaving.

"Our scientists have had one of the first specimens for a few hours now and they think they know how the infection is transmitted," Sergeant Nichols replies.

"I thought it was from being bitten?"

"That too, Major."

"Please tell me it's not airborne," Brooks says.

"Almost as bad, ma'am," the Sergeant answers. "Based on their preliminary tests, our scientists believe the virus can live outside the host for an unusually long period of time. At least hours, maybe days. They also believe it's some new kind of cross between a germ and a parasite. Our boys have named it a *virusite*. According to the brains on our team, a bite isn't the only way it can be transmitted, but it's the most expedient. They also say it can be transferred through mucus membrane contact, and that's the biggest threat."

"Like a venereal disease?"

"Sort of."

"Are you telling me our biggest risk is doggy-sex?" Brooks asks.

"Unprotected sexual contact will definitely transmit the virusite. Either between or across species," he says, pausing to let that sink in. "But, I mean more like the cold wet noses to doggy-buttholes, kind of contact. Anytime one dog meets another, there's a lot of sniffing and licking going on, and that's how they believe it's been spreading so quickly."

"Fuck me," Brooks mutters.

"It gets worse," Nichols continues. "Like I said, the virusite can stay alive outside the host for a period of time. Have you ever seen what a dog does when it's out and there are no other dogs around? Eating scraps from people and other animals. Sniffing over everything as they walk, especially anything left by another animal. And when they come across a single spore of the virusite..." He trails off letting the Major fill in the rest for herself.

"Any other bad news?" Brooks asks, realizing the virus' transmittal acts almost like it's been intentionally designed to behave that way.

"I'm afraid so, ma'am," the Sergeant continues. "As an example. A guy gets up in the morning and cuts himself shaving. He finishes up, gets dressed, pours himself a cup of coffee, and sits down to read the paper or whatever this guy does. But the guy has a dog that's been infected and before the little bastard goes nuclear, it wants one more minute of being man's best friend, jumps on our guy's lap and licks his face where he cut himself earlier. And bingo!"

"Our guy's infected? Without being bitten?" she asks Brooks. She staggers slightly but steadies herself by touching the back of a nearby chair with the tips of her fingers.

"That's what they're saying," he replies, beginning to tick off items with his fingers. "Through the blood. Biting. Mucus membranes to open sores. Ingesting the germ due to poor hygiene. Hell, ma'am. An overzealous doggie-kiss. Maybe stepping in a three-day-old turd in your bare feet with a popped blister, can seal your fate."

"And every infection is fatal..."

"They used to be."

"*Used* to be?"

"The cross-species jump from dogs to other domesticated animals and with the first human victims their brains eventually cooked in their skulls and burned itself out, killing the host. But, when it started spreading from person to person, the infection mutated again."

"The virusite isn't killing them?"

"I didn't say that, ma'am. I'm saying they're not staying dead. Our guys in the labs are reporting the subjects appear to be dying a horribly, painful death caused from the virusite. And then things get weird."

"*Then* things get weird?"

"The corpses are dead as doornails, and then they reanimate..."

"Are you trying to tell me they're becoming zombies?" Brooks asks.

"Not your traditional, *Romero* type of zombies, Major. More like your, *28 Days Later* variety."

"I haven't seen that one," Brooks says.

"They're not shambling drones in the pursuit of brains."

"At least that's one good thing," she replies, feeling slightly relieved things aren't totally lost.

"Actually, ma'am, I think we'd be better off if they were. I'll spare you the details from the movies, but the virusite is making runners out of them. Runners with some degree of problem solving skills left in their burned-out brains. I'm not implying they're solving the equation for time-travel or anything that complicated, but they can use doors, bludgeoning weapons, and have shown some basic combat and attack strategies. Utilizing scouting groups, decoys, that sort of thing."

"Does it take a headshot to bring them down?" Brooks asks, wanting to know what to tell her troops if it should come to that. She knew the movies made it look as simple as the bullets magically finding their targets. But in real life, when your heart is racing and you're constantly moving, it's just not that easy to target the head. It's a relatively simple shot for a trained, calm sniper to hit a slow-moving or stationary target, but that's not a normal combat scenario for most soldiers. Soldiers are always moving, advancing, taking ground. That's why troops are trained to always aim for center-mass. Hit the big target and bring the enemy down by blowing a hole in their torso and letting them bleed out. If the only way to kill the infected was to blow their brains out, she'd have to consider a more cautious strategy.

"It's definitely the most efficient way, but not the only one," Nichols replies. "Most of our troops have been issued M4s. The standard issue 556 round they fire, is definitely going to splatter brains out the back of an infected head. This will immediately drop them. But, so will a bullet to the heart..."

"Thank God," Brooks sighs, finally settling into the chair she'd been holding onto for support.

"I'm not done, ma'am," he says, ticking off fingers again. "And the lungs, liver, and kidneys. You basically have to destroy all the internal organs like you're spraying them with a high-caliber meat grinder."

"Well shit..." Brooks says, realizing this new information changed some of the plans for *Operation Washout*, significantly.

"Our strategists suggest focusing on the legs. Their opinion is, if they can't get to you, they can't infect you. Once they're down, you've got time to use the M4s to put them out of your misery. In my opinion, taking out a knee seems more difficult than a headshot, but that's their recommendation. It's all here in the report the Colonel wanted you to have," he says, handing her a thick, legal-sized envelope.

"The Colonel already has this information?" she asks, taking the envelope from the Sergeant. She turns it over in her hands, thinking there must be an entire ream of paper inside. It's unsealed with the words *Restricted: National Security Clearance Required* printed across both sides. The letters are in black because they only use red in the movies for effect. Brooks has always wondered why they have the warning at all, thinking by advertising, the documents inside immediately became forbidden fruit.

"You seem to know a lot of the information in here," she says.

"Yes, ma'am. I was the one who compiled the report for him. That's his copy," Nichols says, nodding at the package in her hands.

"Before I head to the airstrip..." she says, standing with staccato movements. "I want you to radio ahead and contact Captain Walker."

"What about? Missus Walker?" Nichols asks.

"What?"

"Nothing, Major. Sorry for the interruption," he replies.

"Tell the *Captain*," she continues. "I want the squads to swap out the standard 556s with the 556 hollow-points."

"Good idea, Major. They'll fit the M4s and pack a bigger punch."

"Tell him I want it done before we get there," Brooks adds.

"We, ma'am?" Nichols asks.

"Then grab your gear. You're coming with me. For now, you're the closest thing I have to an expert on this shit," she says, lifting the envelope a little. "And I want you there on the ground with me."

CHAPTER NINE

"I GUESS WE know why the neighborhood streets are empty," Dave says, pulling into the line of slow-moving vehicles that lead to the cluster of freeway onramps. His plan was to hit West 70 to get out of Ohio and then cut north once they were in Indiana and meet up with the boys outside of Gary. Providing they could get a hold of the kids, that is. And after Pam contacted her parents.

"I've tried to call Zack and Ben, and sent them both text messages," Pam says. "I'm going to try my parents, but I'm using the car's Bluetooth. I'm tired of holding this thing to my ear," she adds, tapping her phone screen and causing the Rogue's display screen to come to life. A couple of seconds later, the inside of the car is filled with the sound of a phone ringing. After five rings, the phone picks up.

"Hi. You've reached the Fosters. We can't take your..." Mike Foster's voice begins.

"Damn it!" Pam curses, cutting off her father's recording without leaving a message.

"Was that the house phone?" Dave asks.

"Yeah," she replies, scrolling the phone screen with her thumb.

"Try your mom's cell," he suggests.

"That's where I'm going," she says, a second before the call connects and ringing fills the car again.

"Hi. You've reached Lynn Foster. I can't take your call right now, but if you'd leave..." Pam's mom's voice says before Pam kills the connection with extreme prejudice.

"Did they use a fucking script?" Dave asks, rolling the car forward a few feet.

"Probably," Joe answers from the backseat.

"What are you doing now?" Dave asks Pam.

"Sending her a text," she replies like he really should've known without asking.

Glancing into the rearview mirror, Dave's more than a little shocked to see Joe sliding a loaded magazine into the handle of a pistol and chambering a round.

"Hey! What'cha got there, buddy?" he asks, trying to keep his voice calm and unthreatening.

"It's obviously a gun," Joe replies.

"Where'd you get it?" Dave asks.

"It's the nine-millimeter I bought when I got my concealed carry permit, a year ago," Joe replies. This was the subject of a couple of arguments between him and his mother at that time, and he glances at the back of her head to see her shake it slightly.

"Can I see it?" Dave asks, holding his hand up and carefully watching Joe in the mirror.

"I guess," Joe answers, grabbing the barrel and starting to hand it over, grip first.

Dave pulls his hand back a fraction and asks, "Is the safety on?"

After looking at the gun, Joe reaches up with his other hand and touches the safety, and Dave hears a soft metallic *click*.

"It is now," he says, setting it in Dave's hand.

With great care, Dave checks the safety for himself. When he's satisfied, he leans over, opens the glove box, sets the pistol inside and gently closes it.

"What the heck?" Joe shouts. "I might need that!"

"And if you do, I'll give it back," Dave replies. "But I don't want you to accidentally shoot me in the back while we're in the car!" he says, having had this recurring nightmare more than once since he and Pam met.

"That's not going to happen," Joe protests.

"Not now," Dave agrees, ending the discussion. "Why don't you try your dad's phone?" he asks Pam.

"Please," she replies.

In the age of the handheld computer, better known as smartphones, Mike Foster still uses the original flip-phone he purchased in 2003. He insists he only needs it for making calls, not taking them or sending text messages. Because the thing only has a numerical keypad, all the grandkids agreed with him. Besides the fact it was usually stuffed in his golf bag with a dead battery. Everyone in the family knew to call Lynn on her cell and if they wanted to talk to Mike, they should use the house number.

"Like he ever carries it," Pam says.

"Better safe than sorry," he replies.

"Good point," Joe chimes in.

"Fine," she concedes. "But it'll probably go right to voicemail."

"Like he ever checks that," Joe adds, not helping the situation in the slightest.

A few seconds later they all hear the call and Mike's phone

ringing on the other end of the line. On the second ring, Dave shoots Pam an, *I told you so* expression, causing her to scowl back at him. By the fifth ring, they all expect it to go to voicemail like Pam predicted and they're all shocked when it picks up on the eighth.

"Here!" they all hear Mike say, sounding like he's away from the phone and speaking to someone else. A second later, Lynn comes on the line and Pam motions for everyone in the car to keep quiet.

"Hey sweetie. Thank God you called!" Lynn says.

"Mom! Are you and Mike okay?" Pam asks.

Mike is Pam's stepfather, but he's the guy who helped raise her and was always around when she needed him. During her teens, their relationship had been tenuous, like all teens with their parents, but she loved him just the same and considered him to be her dad. Although, like their own kids, she'd never gotten out of the habit of calling him Mike and he never thought a thing about it.

"We're fine, sort of..." Lynn replies.

"What's wrong?"

"Well... Your father took Apollo out this morning, and everything was fine. He was sniffing around like he usually does. Taking his sweet time doing his business in the yard."

"Mike?" Pam asks, hoping she didn't have to add dementia to their growing list of problems.

"No, honey. Apollo," Lynn replies. "Anyway. A couple hours later, he started acting a little strange, so Mike decided to take him out again. He no sooner got the door open and Apollo turned on him. I've never seen anything like it! He was growling and snarling. Apollo, not your father," Lynn adds.

"So, what did you guys do?"

"The only thing we could do. We ran for the basement and Apollo chased us all the way down."

"Leaving your cell phone on the kitchen counter," Pam says, putting the pieces together.

"Did you try to call? I'm sorry I missed it. You know, I have the same problem when I try to call any of your kids. I think they're..."

"Mom!" Pam shouts, reconsidering the threat of dementia. "Stay with me. Are you guys okay?"

"Like I said. We're fine, but we had to go all the way through the storeroom in the back of the basement before we could get a door closed fast enough to keep Apollo out. The next time I see that vet of ours, and he tells me if Apollo lost some weight he'd be more active, I'm going to tell him a thing or two."

"Mom! Please!" Pam interrupts. "Where are you two now?"

"Still in the basement, sweetie. Apollo was on the other side of the door, trying to chew his way through it, *which we're going to have to paint*." Lynn says the last part away from the phone, the comment being intended for Mike's ears, before continuing. "Your father started piling up anything he could find against the door. I kept telling him the door opens out, but he just kept on stacking. It's a good thing he did though. If he hadn't, his golf bag wouldn't have been on top and we wouldn't have ever heard his phone ring."

"Where's Apollo now?" Dave asks, unable to maintain his silence.

"Hey Dave!" Lynn says. "How you doing, kiddo?"

"Where's Apollo?" he repeats.

"Oh, he's still outside the door. He's not trying to chew through it anymore, but we can still hear him occasionally on the other side. Hey! Why don't I put you guys on speakerphone, so Mike can hear us and we can all talk? *Mike! How do I get this stupid, old thing on speaker?*" Lynn asks away from the phone.

"How do you keep her off of it?" Dave mutters as he creeps into the five-lane, cluster fuck of a freeway interchange.

"Mom! Mom!" Pam shouts.

"Hold on a second, honey," Lynn replies. "Your father is telling me how to do this. *I don't see a button shaped like a speaker... No. You said a button that looks like a speaker, not one with a speaker on it! There's a difference.*"

"Jesus Christ," Dave sighs.

"*Well then, you do it!*" Lynn finally says.

"Pam. Can you hear me?" Mike asks after an excruciating moment of fumbling with the phone.

"Yeah, Mike," she answers.

"Is Dave with you?" he asks.

"I told you he was!" Lynn reminds him.

"He's sitting right next to me, in the car," Pam says.

"Can you put him on the phone?" Mike asks.

"We're on Bluetooth, Mike," she explains.

"So, he can't come to the phone?"

"We're on speakerphone, Grampa," Joe says from the back.

"Hey, sweetie! I didn't know you were there!" Lynn chirps.

Pam hits mute and asks, "Is she talking to me or Joe?"

"The sweetie thing threw me off too," Dakota says before Pam unmutes the mic.

"Hey Gramma," Joe says.

"How you doing, Joe? I haven't talked to you for a while,"

Lynn says as Dave fights the urge to bash his skull against the steering wheel.

"I'm right here, Mike," he says loud enough to end the reunion.

"Hey Dave," Mike replies.

"Is everything alright?"

"For now. Listen. We're stuck down here, and things are going to get bad pretty quickly if Apollo doesn't leave. For starters, there's no bathroom in the storeroom. Only a floor drain. I'm fine with that for now, but Lynn's not happy about it. And, sooner or later, we're going to need something more substantial than a hole with a welded-on drain cover."

"Yeah, but things could be worse," Dave says, trying to make things seem not quite so bad.

"Did I mention we don't have any food or water? Or that this phone is almost dead and there might be another dog with Apollo?"

"And, you've gone right from *Sorta Fucked* to the high end of *Uppercase Fucked*," Dave confirms.

"We could sure use your help," Mike says.

"Mike... We're a hundred and thirty miles from you. It'll take at least two hours to get there in this traffic, if it thins out. Let me think of something."

"Like I said. The battery on this phone isn't going to last mu—"

"Mike! Mom!" Pam shouts.

"Fuck this!" Dave says, pushing the button to engage the all-wheel drive on the Rogue. Turning his right signal on, like a conscientious driver, Dave checks his mirrors and looks to the right to see if there's an opening. The vehicle to their right is a black Escalade, which Dave is certain only comes in that color. The side windows are heavily tinted, making it impossible to see the driver's face, but Dave can see a pair of hands gripping the top of the steering wheel in a white-knuckled grip. Ahead of the SUV is an older, box-type delivery truck with a roll-up door in the back. The Escalade doesn't move when the delivery truck creeps forward, so Dave rolls their car to the right, hoping to capitalize on the asshole's lack of attention and get over another lane before struggling for the next one. But the huge SUV lurches forward at the last second bringing his front bumper even with Dave's front fender.

"What the fuck?" Dave asks no one in particular.

"What an asshole," Joe says, staring at the other driver through his window.

Dave waves a thank you to the guy, playing the politely stupid card, and turns the wheel harder, rolling farther into the guy's lane. The other vehicle jumps forward again, bringing his bumper within inches of the Rogue's door. Dave can see through the windshield and notices the guy sitting motionless as traffic crawls forward again, never looking their direction. Dave can tell through the layers of glass separating them, the man's skin color looks good. His head is lulling forward, but his hands are still gripping the top of his wheel. Dave turns farther, trying to creep in a little more to get past him and into the next lane, suddenly feeling uneasy about the position he's put them all in. When they inch ahead, the guy in the Escalade seems to snap to attention, his eyes locking on their car, and slams into Dave's passenger side. The impact pins the Rogue between the grill of the giant SUV and the box truck on the other side. Dave knows their car is no match for the larger vehicle and sees the box truck's lights flash, indicating the driver has put the damn thing into park and is coming around to investigate the rear end collision.

"Mother fucker!" Dave shouts as Pam and Joe instinctively move away from their doors.

"Look at his face!" Pam yells, pointing through her window.

Inside the Escalade, the driver's face has contorted into an expression of rage. Fluid runs from his eyes and mouth as his teeth gnash together. The guy lets up on the gas and starts jerking violently at his seatbelt trying to free himself from the restraint. At the same time, he's also kicked open his door, driving it into the side of the car that was behind their Rogue, causing that driver to shift into park and open his own door. Apparently, he plans to give Mr. Escalade a piece of his mind but climbs back in and locks his doors when he gets a good look at the berserker clawing at the seatbelt to get to him.

"What the fuck were you thinking, buddy?" the guy driving the box-truck says as he comes around to the back to check for damage. His eyes meet Dave's at the same moment the driver of the Escalade frees himself and jumps out his door, landing on the asphalt like a huge predator. His eyes pass from the car to his left, to the Rogue, and finally lands on the delivery driver who's still outside his vehicle. He starts to scramble trying to figure out a way to get past the obstructions and get to the delivery driver.

"Get back inside your truck and lock the doors!" Dave yells to him as the infected man springs into motion and Dave stomps on his own gas pedal. Metal screams and paint peels off in long curls as Dave tries to force their trapped car between the two larger vehicles.

"You're really messing up your car," Joe says.

"The cop with the wheelchair already scratched the paint, so..." Dave replies. He jerks the wheel back and forth and presses harder on the gas pedal, trying to break free as the tires begin to spin and smoke.

"You hit a cop in a wheelchair?" Dakota asks.

"No! He was *pushing* the wheelchair with a woman in it," Dave says, gritting his teeth as he shifts into reverse, planning to back up to break the hold from the other vehicles.

"You hit a cop, pushing a wheelchair with a woman sitting in it?" Joe asks.

Before Dave can reply, a loud thump comes from the rear passenger end of the Rogue. The berserker from the Escalade is trying to clamber over Dave's bumper, his sights locked on the delivery driver. Dave hits the gas and stomps the brakes a split second later, throwing the guy on his rear bumper off balance and onto the pavement. The guy screams in frustration, slamming his fists onto the blacktop. The delivery driver, having finally put all the pieces together, turns and runs back to the cab of his truck. Horns begin honking from behind them as other drivers, unaware of the shit unfolding at the present, just want to keep moving forward like everyone else. The delivery driver gets to his cab, slams the door closed and lurches forward, trying to escape his closing attacker in the eight feet that's cleared between him and the pickup in front of him. This frees the Rogue and Dave stomps on the gas again, forcing the gap between the vehicles wider as he cuts straight across the two lanes. Glass shatters into the cab of the delivery truck as the infected Escalade driver punches his fist through the safety glass and grabs the terrified driver.

"What are you doing?" Pam asks as Dave bounces his car up and onto the shoulder of the onramp.

"Getting us the fuck out of here! What's it look like?" he replies.

"You'd better buckle up, boys," Pam tells them as she faces forward and braces her hands against the dash. The front of their car bucks as they speed across the shoulder and hit the immense grassy area separating the freeway divisions heading in the four different directions.

"There's another onramp about a mile up. We can probably slip on there and merge into traffic," she tells Dave.

"I've got a better idea," he says. Wrestling with the wheel and angling the bouncing vehicle to the right, Dave heads toward where the lanes for North 71 continue past the interchange.

"Really? Because your right turn signal is still on from your stealthy lane change back there?" she tells him.

"Nah, I've got this," he replies. Flipping the signal off, Dave gives Pam a wink and blows her a kiss as he steers toward the gully passing under 71 on the left, rather than the level ground off to its right.

"Are you sure?" Pam asks, giving up on the dash and grabbing the *oh-shit* handle above her door with both hands.

"I said, I've got this," he repeats with a little less confidence and conviction as they drive down into the gully. The front of the Rogue plows up sections of grass and dirt as they careen down the slope.

"Holy shit!" Dave shouts, cranking the wheel hard to avoid a small group of trees.

"It's not like they just appeared!" Pam shouts. "They're

fucking trees!"

"I thought he was heading for them on purpose," Dakota says, having finally gotten himself and Bongo properly restrained.

"Well, I wasn't," Dave replies, scraping the passenger doors on a low-hanging branch before snapping it off at the trunk.

"Are you sure?" Joe asks, lurching away from his window in case the glass shatters.

"You're fine," Dave assures them as the Rogue starts rolling up the other side of the gully and closer to the freeway. "I told you I had this," he says as he starts to pick up speed.

"What are you doing now?" Pam asks, not releasing her grip on the handle.

"Going to save your folks, babe."

As their vehicle accelerates, Dave drives parallel to the fast lane of North 71, starting to merge in from the left. Traffic is heavy, but it's moving along at around forty as Dave comes over the median edge, like he's skipping the wake from a boat. He paces the traffic, driving along the shoulder and turns on his right blinker, as two military, transport planes bank across the sky over them, swinging around for landing at the Columbus Airport.

CHAPTER TEN

"Major Brooks," Captain Walker says, saluting the senior officer as she exits the back of the military plane. Hers is the last of the transports to land and already her troops from the other three are assembling on the tarmac in formation as the Medium Tactical Vehicles start rumbling in. Three of the MTVs have been fitted for troop transport and the forth has been stripped to carry the extra gear and supplies.

"I'm formally taking command, by orders from Colonel Beaurite," Brooks replies, returning his salute. "This is Sergeant Nichols. He's with me, and if he tells you to jump, consider it an order from me."

"Yes, Major," he replies, standing at attention after giving the Sergeant a curt nod.

"As you were, Captain," she says, allowing her junior officer to stand easy. "I need an update."

"Can I speak freely, Major?" Captain Walker asks, pulling a pack of cigarettes from his camo pockets and fishing out a lighter.

"If it'll save time," Brooks replies as Walker offers her a smoke and she shakes her head, declining the offer.

"I think we're basically deep in the heart of fucked, Major," he says, lighting his smoke and drawing a deep drag.

"Would you like to elaborate Captain, or is that your professional, military appraisal?"

"Yes, and yes," Walker replies, exhaling a lungful of smoke off to the side so he doesn't blow it in the Major's face. "We have dozens of three-man teams, sweeping a twenty-five-mile area around ground zero. That stretches well past the Columbus city limits to the direct southeast and into the surrounding suburbs. And we've got blockades on most of the main roads leading in and out of the area."

"What are the three-man-teams sweeping for?" she asks.

"Things to shoot at, mostly," Walker says. "I've given orders to shoot any stray dog, cat, raccoon or cuddly monkey they come across, on sight. If they see so much as a squirrel, I want it dead."

"What about people they find?" Nichols asks.

"Quarantine," the Captain replies.

"How many do you have so far," Brooks asks.

"In our current holding area, about a thousand which is about two hundred over capacity. We've got some of the National Guard troops busting ass to get more fencing up before the trucks bring more in."

"What are you doing with the infected?" Nichols asks.

"The same," Walker says. "We don't have time to sort them out so we're considering them all to be infected. No friendlies," he adds, crushing his smoke under his boot.

"There won't be if you keep them all confined together," Nichols says.

"Where would you suggest we get the manpower to test them all, Sergeant?" Walker asks, pulling rank without actually coming out and telling Nichols to keep his opinions to himself.

"I don't know, *Captain*," Brooks says, ending the dick measuring before either of them has any more chances of whipping them out. "But are you fucking stupid?" she asks Walker. "If just one person in there is carrying the virusite, they could infect scores before they're discovered. Maybe hundreds."

"And they told two friends... and they told two friends..." Nichols mutters.

"Can it, Sergeant!" Brooks snaps. "Captain. Take a team of your men, I don't care where in the hell you get them from, and start sorting the ones you have."

"Sorting them, how... Major?" Walker asks.

"Sergeant Nichols..." she says, gesturing with her open hand in a, *be my guest* fashion.

"For starters, we need someplace bigger," Nichols says.

"We've started preparing to commandeer the soccer stadium as another location. We can hold about twenty thousand in the seats alone, and double that if we're forced to," Captain Walker replies.

"Good," says the Sergeant. "Divert all future civilians the teams come across to there. It won't hold them all for long, but forty thousand gives us a little breathing room, for now. Then start with the ones you already have and sort them out. Weed out the ones who're obviously infected," he continues, not trying to keep the, *you fucking idiot* tone out of his voice. "This means anyone with bad color, bite marks or even scratches. But also, anyone showing signs of illness or fever. This thing is a distant relative of rabies and temperatures will spike for anyone infected. Oh! And keep your eyes open for anyone who looks out of place."

"Out of place, how?" the Captain asks as he and Brooks turn to look at Sergeant Nichols.

"Out of place, like a lion in a group of gazelles. Anyone who looks more predator then detainee. Keep an eye on those fuckers and we can weed them out if we're forced to. Send everyone who looks clean to the stadium and institute the same process there. No one gets in who doesn't look clean. Everyone else gets red-flagged."

"And what do we do with them?" Walker asks.

"Consider them all cuddly monkeys," Major Brooks says. "But before you do any of that, make sure my troops are loaded and ready to go. We roll out of here in five. Then contact the Colonel and tell him I'm preparing to initiate *Operation Washout*. I'll inform him of my final decision after I've had a chance to survey the surrounding areas and determine what the breach ratio is."

"Breach ratio?" the Captain questions. "I already said we have most of the major roads covered."

"Most doesn't mean all the main roads. And it sure as hell doesn't come close to covering all the smaller ones. We took a flyover of the area before landing, and all your blockades are doing is forcing the escaping infected to the side streets. You can't just shut down some of them. It's all or nothing, Captain. You should have bottled them up on the freeways while you had the chance and just rolled in to gather them up. But you decided to half-ass it, so here we are, and that's why you're no longer in charge. Now, before carrying out your other orders, have someone get the Sergeant and I a cup of hot coffee," she adds, making sure with her final order, Walker has no question about who's in charge and where *he* sits on the ladder.

"Would either of you like cream and sugar with that, Major Brooks?" the Captain asks, biting back his contempt and anger.

"Fresh and black with be fine," she replies.

"Wow!" Nichols says after Walker storms away. "I was kind of a dick to him, but you cut the son of a bitch in half. We'll be lucky if he doesn't spit in our coffees."

"I hate lifers like him," Brooks says, glaring at the Captain's back. "He's in it for the career opportunities, like the U.S. Army is the world's biggest Walmart. He probably spends more time commanding the PX than he does the rest of his troops."

"I ran the PX back at Bolivar for three years," Nichols tells her.

"And I'm sure you did a damn fine job of it," she replies, turning to face him with a practiced, but fake smile. "Get our gear into one of the MTVs. I'll meet you there after I check on the troops. You'll ride up front with me. I want you there when I finally get a look and see how fucked up this Hilliard place is."

CHAPTER ELEVEN

DAVE KEEPS THEM going north on 71 for over an hour, weaving through traffic when he can, trying to make better time to Canton. When they reach the Highway 30 exit that heads northeast to Canton, Pam and Joe clutch the *oh-shit* handles over their heads as they hit the thirty-mile and hour, sweeping right turn at fifty. The tires screech in protest as Dakota is forced into his door. He tries to keep Bongo from being crushed between them as the excited dog bounces from his lap to Joe's. Realizing he might be going a little fast, Dave lifts his foot from the gas but avoids using the brake. Everyone relaxes as they straighten out, and Bongo gives a *yip* from the back. Dave's gaze flashes to the rearview mirror as the hot breath hits his neck and he freezes, certain the dog has turned like he'd predicted and is about to rip out his throat. A wet tongue runs up his neck as Bongo licks his appreciation for the best car ride ever, and a chance to play *king of the backseat* with his owners. The dog looks back at him in the mirror and Dave would almost swear he's smiling. His dripping tongue hangs from his mouth as he pants rapidly. His eyes are clear and bright as Bongo's tail smacks Joe and Dakota with delight.

"Get him off me," Dave says. Not wanting to take his hands from the wheel, he wipes the slobber from his neck by tipping his head to the right and using his shoulder.

They drive another forty-five minutes before the inside of the Rogue is flooded again with the sound of a ringing phone and Dave glances at the display on the dash. His stomach tightens as he sees who's calling him and punches the button on the steering wheel to accept the call.

"Brigette? Where's Zack? Are you guys okay?" he asks.

"He's right here next to me in the car and we're all fine," Brigette answers.

"Sorry, Dad," Zack shouts from a few feet away.

"Yeah, I've accidentally had my phone on silent this whole time and Zack's is dead. We've got it on the charger while we're driving," he explains.

"You're driving? So, you've got Ben?" Dave asks hopefully.

"Not exactly."

"What the fuck does that mean?" Pam asks.

"While we were doing everything you guys told us to do, and getting Jaxon and Braxton ready, Zack was trying to get ahold of him and we didn't notice when his phone died. Once we realized his was dead we plugged it in and Ben sent back a text. He said he was going to check on Mike and Lynn and he'd meet us there."

"Shit!" Dave barks. "How long ago was that?"

"Less than five minutes ago. We're on our way and should be there in about thirty minutes," Brigette answers. "Where are you guys?"

"We're headed there too," Dave replies. "Apollo has them trapped in the basement. But we're only about fifteen minutes out, so we'll get there before you and hopefully Ben. We'll try to sort out the shit with Apollo," he continues, glancing at the shotgun. "But we might wait for you all to get there first. Make sure your gun is loaded when you get there."

"Already done and in my lap," Brigette assures him. She'd spent some time in the military before meeting Zack and she seems to be slipping back into the conditioned mindset.

"Mike says there might be more than one dog in the house," Dave warns.

"Can he confirm?" Brigette asks.

"No. His phone's dead. It's only by luck we got ahold of them at all. Look, if something happens and you guys get there before us, wait for me to get there before you try going in," Dave says.

"Will do, Dave. And sorry about the phones," she says.

"Just keep them on and turned up from here on out. We'll see you when you get there," he replies.

"Roger that. Be safe," Brigette says before ending the call.

"Fucking kids..." Dave mutters, glancing in his mirror at their own panting time bomb in the back seat, as he presses harder on the accelerator and weaves through traffic.

Seventeen minutes later, they're off the freeway and pulling on to Mike and Lynn's street. Their house sits on a large corner lot in the upscale neighborhood. Most of the homes in their subdivision are oversized brick or stone Tudors with large, well-groomed yards. Theirs has one of the few driveways that pass in front of the house. One end opens to the street that passes the southern end of the lot. The other enters from the west side and splits with one direction leading to the large parking area in front of their two-car garage and the other completing the connection to the southern entrance. This allows vehicles to drive past the front of the house to deliver the paper, daily mail, or whatever. The main and upper floors of their two-story, brick home has two dining areas, a kitchen Dave always envied, three huge bedrooms, a number of bathrooms and a formal living room. The basement level has a den, with two leather recliners positioned in front of a large television where the Fosters spend their evenings watching recordings of golf matches and their favorite shows. There's also a workshop down there where Mike tinkers around with home projects, and a series of separate, unfinished storerooms, which Dave and Pam have always referred to as the *catacombs*. It's in there, where the couple is trapped behind a hollow, interior door, by at least one dog.

Dave drives slowly along the street the house faces, planning to enter the west end of the driveway and park in front of the front doors. But, there's a mail truck parked there with its flashers on, as if the mailman had stopped to drop off a package just moments before they arrived. The rolling, white box with the USPS logo on the side, blocks a complete view of the front door but allows enough over the top, for them to see it's standing open. Dave stops the car in the street and watches for any signs of movement from within the house. He can't be certain, but it looks like the van isn't running.

"Maybe Apollo took off when the mailman showed up and he's already let them out of the basement?" Joe asks, staring out his window.

"Then someone would have come out, or something," Dave says.

"What are you waiting for?" Pam asks, anxious to check on her parents.

"I'm just looking for... I don't know. Something."

"Like what?" she asks.

"Like where the hell is everybody? Usually there's at least a few kids playing in one of the yards or a random jogger, or even another car... But look at this place. It's not quite four o'clock in the afternoon on a Saturday and the neighborhood looks deserted."

"Someone's in the house across the street," Dakota says.

"How do you know?" Joe asks.

"I saw someone pull the curtain back a few inches when we pulled up, but no one's shown their faces. I don't know if they're still watching us or not, but I know what I saw."

Dave follows where Dakota is looking but doesn't see anyone either. He looks at the next house down on that side of the street and sees the curtains inside its large front windows are sagging in tatters. He sits for a full minute, shifting his attention from watching the front of Mike and Lynn's house to scanning the homes across the street. "Screw it..."

Lifting his foot from the brake, he turns right and rolls down the driveway. He turns right again, pointing them at the front of the mail truck parked in front of the house, its yellow hazard lights blinking at them. Like the front door to the house, he sees the sliding driver's door on the right side of the small box-truck is standing open. Dave shifts into reverse and takes a few seconds to quietly back around the end of the house, parking in front of the closed garage doors and pointing the Rogue back the way they came in.

"Just in case," he tells Pam.

They sit for several seconds, listening to the cooling engine tick before Pam asks, "What now?"

"I guess I go in," Dave answers, grabbing the twelve-gauge from next to his seat.

"I want to go too," she says.

"I don't think so," he replies. "Let me go in and look around. If Apollo's gotten to your parents, I want to cover them up before you come in. If he hasn't chewed through the door yet, and he's still in there, I'm going to have to kill him. The fewer people in there when the shooting starts, the better."

"What if he has gotten to them and they're like the guy in the park or the one from the onramp?" Pam asks.

"Yeah..." he replies, his grip tightening on the barrel.

"Let me go with you," Joe says.

"I was planning on it," he tells him as he pops open the glove box and pulls out the pistol from inside.

Dave checks the safety again before handing it over the seat to Joe. Out of reflex, Joe pops the magazine out and checks it before sliding it back into the grip. Then he pulls the slide back to be certain there's already a round in the chamber.

"I have the shotgun, so I'm going in first and you're staying right behind me," Dave tells him. "I'll take care of anything that comes at us from the front. You only have two jobs. The first is to make sure nothing sneaks up behind us, understood?"

"Understood," Joe nods. "What the other one?"

"Don't fucking shoot me," he answers. "You two wait here for us. We'll be back in a few minutes, but just in case, I want you to climb into the driver's seat when I get out," he tells Pam.

"What about me?" Dakota asks.

"Keep Bongo under control and do whatever Pam tells you to do," Dave says. "Are you ready, Joe?"

"No," he answers, pushing his safety to off and opening his door.

"I love you, baby," Pam tells Dave as he exits the Rogue and she ungracefully climbs over the center console.

"I love you, too. See you in a few minutes," he says, giving her a kiss on the lips before pushing his door closed without slamming it shut.

"Is your safety off?" Joe asks in a whisper.

"It is now," Dave answers. "We're not going to rush through this. We check the mail truck first and then the house. Once we're inside, we close the front door so nothing can come in behind us. Then we clear the living and dining rooms before we head to the kitchen. After that, we'll move upstairs and check the bedrooms and office. We make sure to look under tables, desks, and beds, any place a dog can hide, and we do one room at a time. Every room we clear, we leave the door open. The catacombs are last."

"If Apollo's still in there, won't he have heard us moving around by then?"

"I hope so. I don't want to get down to the basement and have to shoot at him while he's standing in front of the door Mike and Lynn might still be hiding behind."

"Good point," Joe says.

"I thought so," Dave replies in a whisper. "You check the truck."

They make their way closer to the open door of the mail truck with the warning lights still flashing and Dave keeps the barrel of the shotgun leveled at the front door of the house. He eases to his left so Joe can come around his right and look inside. The cab is empty and the door to the back where the mail is kept has been slid open. Joe pulls the hammer back on his nine-millimeter and takes the short step up into the cab. He leans around the corner and checks the back. There're several empty totes used for holding the daily envelopes, packages and junk mail, stacked in the back. A couple are still full and sitting on the racks mounted to the inside walls. Other than that, the truck is empty.

"It's empty," he says, taking the next step inside and standing next to the driver's seat.

"What are you doing?" Dave asks. Without taking his eyes from the front door, he backs up a step and presses his back against the side of the engine compartment. Partly to see if the engine is still warm but mostly to have something solid behind him.

"Turning off the flashers. They're creeping me out," Joe replies.

"The engine's cold," Dave says.

"So...? Oh..."

"Come on," Dave says, edging away from the van and moving closer to the door. "Remember," he whispers. "Do not shoot me."

"I know," Joe whispers back.

The sky is overcast and at this time of year, in the autumn afternoon, the light to their backs spills in through the open doorway but leaves the rest of the interior in darkness. Dave keeps the shotgun tracking where his eyes go as he steps into the doorway, pausing to let his eyes adjust to the light before entering. Joe follows him through and silently closes the front door behind them. The entry is clear and the dining and sitting areas to their right are deserted. There's a sparse trail of envelopes and flyers leading behind the large marble-top counter that separates the kitchen from the table and chairs Mike and Lynn usually sit at to eat their meals or sip coffee in the mornings. Dave checks under the table before following the trail of letters around the end of the counter. Joe follows but has his back to Dave's, keeping his pistol aimed at the landing of the stairs that lead up to the bedrooms and down to the catacombs. The door to the half-bathroom, just to the other side of the landing is closed. It's really more of a deep closet with a toilet and sink in it, but it's more convenient during family gatherings or when the Fosters are entertaining friends, than the other three full bathrooms on the other floors.

"You better see this," Dave whispers to Joe, turning away from the horror on the floor.

Joe feels Dave's hand on his shoulder, turning him toward the kitchen as Dave steps in front of him to cover the stairs. The first thing Joe sees are a pair of legs, covered in the traditional, blue uniform pants of the U.S. Postal Service, sprawled on the floor. He takes another step and the whole picture comes into view. He'd been trying to prepare himself for what they might find in the house and expected to see the mailman. But it was a mail woman lying on the floor. A pool of dark blood surrounds the upper half of the postal carrier's body and has already begun to congeal. There are a few bite marks on her arms and dried blood leaves small trails from the punctures. But that's not the source of the sticky puddle her body is laying in. The right side of the woman's neck has been ravaged, along with the side of her face. The carnage starts in her shoulder, at the base of the neck, and runs up the right side of her face. Large chunks of flesh have been torn free, leaving short ribbons of bloody meat clinging around the edges. There aren't any pieces laying in the puddle, like grotesque little islands in a tiny sea of thickening crimson, so they must have been eaten. The skin and muscle from around her jawline has been chewed away, leaving her molars and jaw bone fully exposed. Joe gags when he sees a fly land, and then scamper across her open, milky-dead eye.

"That's just about the grossest thing I've ever seen," he whispers, wiping the back of his free hand across his mouth. "Thanks for sharing that."

"I try. Follow me," Dave whispers.

Stepping around the body, being careful not to step in the coagulating pool, they creep to the door on the other side of the kitchen, leading to the garage. They hold their breaths as Dave silently turns the knob and pulls the door open. He immediately pans the gun across the floor. Going left to right and back to the left again, making sure there's nothing close to the door. Both cars are parked inside and Dave motions for Joe to look under the one on the left while he does the same with the one on the right. When they're both satisfied there's nothing under the vehicles, other than floor, they walk as far around each of them as they can before returning to the center of the garage.

"Do you think Apollo killed that woman?" Joe asks.

"I don't think it was a squirrel. Let's keep going."

They move back into the kitchen, avoiding the dead woman on the floor, and move to the landing. There are four steps going up to the hallway that has an office on the left and the master bedroom at the end. At the top of the steps, another set of carpeted stairs go up again, leading to the two oversized bedrooms upstairs. They move directly down the hall first, finding the small office space empty, other than the usual clutter Mike and Lynn have been slowly collecting in there for years. The bedroom door is open slightly and Dave uses the barrel to push it the rest of the way while Joe covers their backs. Dave checks the room is clear before having Joe enter as he opens the door to the master bathroom and verifies it's empty.

"I fucking hate this," Dave whispers, patting his pockets for the cigarettes he left in the car.

"I wish I would have stayed in the car with Mom," Joe replies.

"Me too," Dave says, not bothering to explain if he was referring to Joe or himself. "Come on."

They go back down the hall, turning left up the stairs to search the two bedrooms and the bathroom between them. All three rooms are vacant.

"I thought you said Apollo would hear us by now?" Joe says quietly.

"If he's in the house, he must have by now. We're not as loud as a marching band or anything, but we're talking about a dog's sense of hearing."

"Then where the heck is he?" Joe asks.

Dave doesn't reply as they both feel the dread sink in with the thought of Apollo waiting down in the basement for them, hiding in a dark corner of the catacombs.

"Only the basement's left," Dave says, trying to shake the persistent image from his mind.

"Uh-huh," Joe agrees. "We're going down there, aren't we?"

"Like we've got a choice," Dave replies, resigned to the deed.

They double check each room again as they pass them, making certain they haven't missed any rabid beasts or killer clowns hiding in the closets. At the bottom of the landing, they steel their resolves and move down into the first room of the basement. The recliners are in their usual spots, but one of the end tables has been knocked over, presumably during the Fosters frantic race to escape their loyal Apollo. The lamp that usually sits on the table is on the other side of the room, broken against the wall. Dave wonders if Mike might have tried hitting the dog with it in their scramble to safety. The door leading to the workshop and the other storage rooms is wide open, but all the lights are off back there, and the dark void is silent.

"It's pretty quiet down there," Dave whispers, keeping his barrel aimed at the open door.

"A little too quiet," Joe replies with a nervous chuckle.

"Knock it off," Dave tells him as he advances cautiously on the doorway, expecting Apollo to leap out of the darkness with each step he takes.

With one hand holding the pistol grip of the shotgun, he uses his other to feel around for the light switch he knows is just on the other side of the door. His fingers finally feel the familiar switch and he flips it on. Fluorescent tube lights spasm to life, lighting up the workshop area and down the narrow hallway. The workshop is open, so they check and clear that room first as quietly and quickly as possible, before following the path of open doors leading farther into the basement. They check the bathroom to the left of the workshop and keep moving down the passage. There's another open door, separating the three other storage rooms from the rest of the house at the end of the confining hallway. Mike and Lynn have to be in one of these. The floor is bare cement and the walls are unfinished brick. A smattering of cobwebs near the ceiling and around the exposed floor joists for the upper floor completes the foreboding look and sends a chill up Dave's spine. He's seen way too many horror movies where some stupid college kid goes into this exact same scene to check a fuse, or investigate a strange noise. His final words to his partying friends are always the same, before culling himself from the herd. *I'll be right back.*

As they get closer to the door, Dave struggles to remember where the light switch is that illuminates these other rooms. He keeps waiting to see a savage monster lunge for his throat from out of the darkness, but there's nothing but dead silence on the other side of the doorway.

"Do you smell that?" Joe asks, pulling up the neck of his T-shirt to cover his nose.

"How could I not?" Dave replies, fighting to control his gorge.

"What is it?"

"I guess we'll find out. Do you want to go first?"

"And break away from your plan? Are you kidding?" he asks, giving Dave a small push toward the door with his elbow.

"I hate you," Dave says, inching closer to whatever is waiting for them inside.

Blindly sliding his hand up and down the inside wall, Dave begins to panic when he can't find the light switch until Joe reminds him it's on the left side of the door. After changing tactics, Dave immediately finds the switch and flips it up. Another set of fluorescent bulbs flicker on, revealing the source of the horrendous smell.

At first, neither of the men are certain what they're looking at and it takes a moment for Dave's mind to wrap itself around the idea. On the floor, in front of door number three to the left, is the motionless body of what was once Apollo. The difficult part to come to grips with is the condition of the remains. It reminds Dave of a bug splattered against a windshield, only the dog's body is still relatively intact. But it looks like every part of the animal's body, intended to keep its insides from coming outside, just gave up. There's a drying spray of blood from its mouth across the cement. More of the stuff leaks from its ears and the eyes and nose have streams of mucousy fluid running from them. A mixture of shit, blood and possible postal carrier has erupted from the dog's ass, staining the floor a dark color and probably destroying the home's resale value forever with the stink.

"Get a blanket from the other room," he tells Joe, no longer bothering to whisper.

"Dave? Is that you?" Mike calls from behind the closed door.

"It's me," he replies. "Stay there. We need to clean up a little bit before you come out."

"Is Apollo out there?"

"That's what we're cleaning up."

"Could you kind of hurry up," Lynn says.

"Do you have an appointment or something," Dave asks.

"No. But I'd kind of like to use the bathroom within the next minute or two," his mother-in-law replies.

"Going as fast as we can, Mom," he assures her as Joe returns with the blanket. They opt for wiping up as much of the floor detritus as they can with the blanket, being careful not to get any of the gore on them. Then they use it to wrap Apollo and drag him from in front of the door. With the path clear, Dave pulls the door open and an avalanche of various things people store for decades comes tumbling through the opening, nearly knocking Dave on his ass. He stumbles backward, trying to avoid being buried and remembers the safety is still off on the shotgun. Before Mike and Lynn can make it out of the room, he and Joe have their safeties on and the guns pointed at the ground.

"Hey sweetie," Lynn says as she climbs over the pile of debris to get to the bathroom in the hall. "Thanks for coming," she adds as she closes the door.

"What she said," Mike says.

Tossing a couple of golf bags aside to make a clearer path out from the storeroom, he walks up to Dave and the two men embrace. Pulling away, Mike gives Joe the same hug before looking at the large lump under the blanket.

"Apollo?" he asks soberly and Dave nods. "Did you have to..."

"He was like this when we got down here," Dave says, not making his father-in-law finish the question.

"I wondered what that smell was," Mike says, wrinkling his nose. "At first, I was going to ask Lynn, but I'm sure you know how well that would've gone over."

"I married her daughter, so... yeah."

"Right. So, I just did my best to ignore it until she said something about it. I figured if it was her, she wouldn't say a word."

"Not even an apology?" Joe asks.

"Probably not," Mike replies. "I'm sure she farted a couple times while we were stuck in there, but I didn't want to call her on it and start an argument I couldn't stomp away from."

"What is that awful smell?" Lynn asks a moment later, exiting the bathroom and closing the door quickly behind her.

"Let's all go upstairs," Dave says, avoiding the debate.

"Then what?" Mike asks.

"Then we load up one of your cars with as much non-perishable food as you have and we wait for the others to get here," he says.

"The others?" Lynn asks.

"Zack and Brigette should be here with the boys any minute. Ben is supposed to be on his way here and might already be outside with Pam and Dakota."

"Should I make everyone a sandwich or something?" she asks.

"I don't think you're going to want to make any food in the kitchen," he tells her. "There's a body lying in a pool of blood behind the counter."

"Who is it?" Lynn asks.

"Evidence points to the mail lady."

"Oh, Betty... She was always so nice," Lynn laments.

"We heard some commotion and crashing coming from up there," Mike says. "We were both hoping it wasn't one of you."

"I'm so glad it wasn't," Lynn adds.

"Me too," Joe agrees as the four of them step out of the catacombs and into the television room with the recliners.

"What the fuck ever," Dave mutters, leading them to the stairs. "Joe, go outside and bring your mom and Dakota in. Tell her that her parents are fine and keep your eyes open."

"Should I go through the garage?" Joe asks as he starts up ahead of the others.

"No. It takes way too long for the garage door to open and close. Use the front door, the way we came in. That way, we can close it quickly if we have to," Dave says as he follows Joe to the door and leans the twelve-gauge in the corner. He doesn't want to keep carrying it around and he definitely doesn't want to accidentally forget it when they finally leave. "And keep your eyes open while you're out there!"

"I was gonna," Joe replies, checking outside before closing

the door behind him.

"Hey, Dave?" Mike calls from the kitchen.

"I know, Mike. Let me grab a blanket from the back of the loveseat to cover up the body," Dave says, certain Mike and Lynn would prefer not to look at the gruesome remains on their floor.

"Thanks," Mike says.

Dave walks from the front door to the sitting area next to the formal dining table. He keeps his eyes on his in-laws to make sure the disturbing image doesn't freak them out or send them into shock. To his surprise, they both look relatively calm. If Dave had to put a word to it, he'd say they look confused. Maybe it's not dear Betty.

"Have you been drinking?" Mike asks. "Because there's no body in the kitchen."

"Wha..." Dave starts to ask as he's hit from behind and sent sprawling across the floor.

To be continued...

Made in the
USA
Lexington, KY